ALIEN PRINCE CHARMING

A Sci-Fi Alien Fairy Tale Romance

ZARA ZENIA

Illustrated by
NATASHA SNOW

Edited by
VALORIE CLIFTON

CONTENTS

CHAPTER 1

GARDAX

I cleared my throat, pinched the bridge of my nose, and for the third time, inhaled deeply. The many eyes of my brothers were upon me. I braced myself as I prepared to upend their lives. You could hear a pin drop into the abyss of silence swirling through the room, but the quiet would soon come to a crashing and abrupt end.

In any lifetime, there comes a point where one is called to measure up, to rise to the occasion and do what we must to become the person we were meant to be. I was about to ask that of my brothers, and more to the point, myself.

"For the love of Trilynia, do you plan to explain sometime tonight why you've summoned us here, Gardax?" Rawklix asked, rolling his bright blue eyes.

The rest of my brothers grumbled their own muted impatience. Rawklix, the youngest at 18, was still callow enough to give voice to his impudent complaints.

"Mind your place, little one," warned Manzar, squaring his jaw and leveling Rawklix with an icy stare that begged to be challenged.

Rawklix lifted one side of his mouth into a smirk. "Always such a foul mood, Manzar! You need to take a trip to my islands. If you'd tasted the pleasures of paradise, you might not be so content to sit around scratching your balls. Regardless, I have better things to be doing, and they involve naked women, so if you don't mind hurrying this little reunion along, I'd be quite grateful." He drummed his long fingers on the table as if his patience were wearing thin and he were warning us of an impending repercussion to that fact.

The massive square muscles of Manzar's shoulders tensed, so I held up my hand, stemming the violence before it began. I knew a brewing fight when I saw one, and I had neither the time nor the energy to feed into these men's egos.

Manzar was a military man and nearly as adept a warrior as myself. Rawklix stood no chance against him, but more importantly, there were matters far more pressing than the posturing egos of my younger brothers. They could clash at each other's throats on their own time.

"Enough, both of you. Bloody each other on your own time. I will not keep you here long, for obvious reasons, but for now, Trilynian business takes precedence, and you will all sit and hear what I have to share with you," I said, gaining the attention of all six of my brothers. My voice boomed and barreled through the room, crashing down upon them like waves pelting the sand.

I nodded to Coel, my burly guardsman, and he silently swung open the thick metal door that was the only way in or out of the council room. The room was heavily fortified and operated on its own power source, completely distinct from the rest of the palace, making it the most secure space and ideal for such a conference. If you needed to discuss private matters, the council room was where you could operate under the most discrete of circumstances.

A few seconds later, in marched my two top scientists, looking a bit bewildered by the company before them. It was clear by their rattled expressions that they hadn't been expecting the entire council to be together in this situation.

The viral outbreak that had ravaged Trilynia had resulted in tight precautions that meant my brothers and I were rarely in the same location at once, the risks of infection too grave. Everyone had to be under tight lock and security. There was no room for error in the world we now lived in.

"Your Highnesses," Lifiya, the lead researcher said, dropping to the floor and kowtowing beside her assistant, a thin man, at least by Trilyn standards, with messy brown hair and anxious eyes. She awaited a command or response before lifting her head.

"Please rise. I do not wish to be burdened with ceremony. Proceed with your presentation." I strained not to let my failing attitude in the moment leak through my voice, but it was a nearly impossible challenge.

"Of course, Your Highness." She nodded, blinking owlishly. "Please forgive my surprise. I assumed this would be a remote conference," she said, setting the small box in her faintly trembling hands on the table before us. Her eyes briefly flickered across the table, skirting from brother to brother with subtle apprehension.

Pressing her hand into the gooey biometric scanning port, she unlocked and opened it, lifting the small metal device in front of her face. Now, she had stoic determination and precise concentration reflecting in her features.

"Your Graces, may I present you with our prototype Biostatistical Information Assessment and Symbiosis Scanner," she said reverently, staring at the item like it contained the secret to life itself. The pride radiating from her aura as she displayed the object was remarkable and unmatchable.

"We call it the BIAS scanner," added her assistant, looking eager to participate. She shifted her weight and licked her lips, eyeing each of us as if she were proud of her contribution to the conversation.

"A dubious acronym," my younger brother Jinurak responded, his twin Lortnam nodding in agreement. They seldom exchanged a difference of opinion.

Lifiya flashed an irritated look at her assistant then offered the device to me. It was weightier than I expected. I held it in my palms and gave it a thorough inspection.

"Dubious as it may sound, this will ensure the future of our people," I announced, passing it to Darbnix who sat nearest me. "Be careful," I advised. "Don't drop it."

The small blue watch-lizard on his shoulder scrambled down and inspected the device as he did. How he could be so comfortable with the tiny reptile crawling on him was beyond me. The lizard curled its prickly red tongue out of its snarly little mouth. Its eyes narrowed with curiosity and it cocked its head to the side.

Lifiya seemed to tense nervously and reached out before stopping herself. "It's our only model so far, though we will have the others completed soon." Her voice was raspy and squeaky at the same time. She eyed the lizard with weary caution as she spoke.

"And? What does it do?" Rawklix asked, still looking bored and impatient. He rolled his eyes and let out a deliberately large and long-winded sigh, leaning back in his chair.

"It scans the genetic markers and biocomposition of an organism to identify compatibility between two specimens. A device will be created for each of Your Highnesses and programmed to each of your unique genetic configurations. Once formatted, the scanner can accurately detect the reproductive compatibility of any specimen surveyed and identify the individual whose markers offer optimal genetic potential for the production of viable progeny, your perfect match."

"In other words, my brothers, meet our new match-makers. There will be no more delay in acquiring a bride for any of us," I said solemnly, feeling the weight of the matter acutely myself. My emotions on the subject were still floating up in the air and up for debate.

A hush fell over the room as the moment sank in. It was true. We were each of us well-acquainted with our mission. The future of our race depended upon our success in locating human mates, who were, incredibly, immune to the virus which had devastated our race, and producing virally resistant offspring. We were out of resources, out of options.

"And what qualifies as a 'perfect match'?" Darbnix inquired, popping the knuckles of his large dark hands, an expression of concern crossing his face. He frowned skeptically. The watch lizard on his arm had returned to its post at his shoulder, tensing nervously as it mimicked the apprehension of its master. Its huge glassy eyes harbored slits for pupils that dilated when the creature engaged in anxiety of any kind.

Lifiya chewed her lip for a moment before continuing. Perhaps it might have been a nervous habit. Perhaps it was the pressure of promoting the device.

"What we have concerned ourselves with in this

endeavor was genetic compatibility—locating an individual with whom you'll have the most success in producing healthy offspring. I understand that there are other factors involved in the mating process . . ." She trailed off as she assessed the response and reaction of the assembly in front of her.

Darbnix gave a humorless laugh that was laced with palpable cynical flair.

"However, such matters are certainly not the province of science," she finished. I noticed how her throat moved as she took a hard swallow.

"So, you're saying that this trifling gadget" —Rawklix gestured at the scanner, which was now on the glass-like surface of the table before us— "could match us with a warty, bearded pit-dweller and we'll have no choice but to bed them?"

The unease rolled through each of my brothers at the notion that their choice of future bride was now left so blindly to science. The scenario didn't sit well with any of us, and I mentally stewed in my seat, stoically adhering to serenity. I wanted to fully understand the device and how it worked before I made any knee-jerk conclusions.

Suddenly, Darbnix let loose a loud laugh, the force of it sending his lizard scrambling up to perch in Darbnix's short brown hair. "Don't get ahead of yourself, boy. As wet behind the ears as you are, Rawklix, you should be happy for any woman who will take you." It was common for him to playfully tease his brother in a patronizing way.

"Perhaps I should stick to animals then, like you, Darbnix?" Rawklix sneered. He was always easily defensive. Quippy retorts came naturally to him, and I found them at the very least amusing as long as I wasn't the one facing the backlash.

Darbnix barely registered the insult, but the little lizard on his arm shimmered to a brilliant fiery red and launched itself at Rawklix, hissing and biting as he struggled to shake free of it. The little creature was feisty and animated as it enthusiastically thrashed on top of Rawklix.

"*Argh!* Call off your vile little worm!" Rawklix shouted, spitting as his hair became askew and disheveled in the struggle. His cheeks burned bright red with fresh fury.

Laughing, Darbnix reached out and grabbed the lizard by the tail. "Come, Vigo, let the boy and his wounded ego alone. We wouldn't want to scratch that pretty face, after all." The lizard emitted a strange clicking, shimmering back to blue, and settled on

Darbnix's arm. It perched there with smug satisfaction.

I stood. "Enough squabbling. Rawklix—all of you —*this* is our duty. It doesn't matter what we sacrifice in the process. We must do what is right by our planet and by our people. The seven of us are the best chance of survival for Trilynia. If that means you must compromise your shallow standards, Rawklix, then you will do so without complaint, for there are far greater consequences at stake." My voice left little room for debate. This was a somber subject, but I wasn't going to stand idly by as I watched my planet deplete of living beings who no longer had the ability to procreate.

"And what is so wrong with satisfying my own standards in a mate as well as those demanded of me by Trilynia? I'm perfectly capable of finding a woman. Why must I obey some gadget?" Rileen was confrontational and morose. He always asked questions. He never took no for an answer.

"There are 14 billion humans on Earth, and roughly half of those are females. Divided evenly among us, that is still approximately one billion human women for each of us to weed through," I answered patiently so that he would finally see the point. "Under ideal circumstances, we would all have the freedom to select the mate of our choice, but these are not those circumstances. We have had more than enough time to find brides in the typical way and none of us has done so. Results are due now, and it is our responsibility to deliver. Having the choice taken from you . . . well, I don't expect any of you to be happy about the situation, but I do expect you to honor your duties," I finished soberly.

No one contradicted me, even Rawklix, as we all thought back to the state of our home planet two dwarf stars away. I was the eldest brother. In the end, I was the established voice of reason. I had the final say in decisions made around this council table.

Life managed to continue on there, even with the looming threat of extinction, but we all knew that matters would not remain peaceful for long if we did not send word back soon of our success in locating mates. The people of this planet would be hunting for answers, and it was me and my brothers they would be looking to.

The Great Plan had been conceived by the Royal Council in one of the darkest hours of Trilynian history. The virus that had swept through our people had rendered the majority of our women infertile, and without the promise of a future, chaos had threatened to unravel the very fabric of our society.

Panic rippled through the communities like a Tsunami wreaking havoc and flooding the areas around its destructive path.

Our expedition, the chance that we might be able to ensure the next generation of Trilyns, had reignited some small spark of hope. Hope might seem a trifling, sentimental notion, but without it, the worst of society emerged. Anger erupted in people's minds. Chaos ensued. There were many protests.

"You are right, of course, Gardax," Manzar, ever loyal, agreed. If I ever needed a right-hand man, he was the one I turned to. He was the one I could trust under any taxing situation.

"We'll need some sort of system for this," Lortnam added contemplatively. Among my brothers, his mind was the one most suited toward matters of organization and resource management. He was the type to always process and digest information and then carefully and measuredly come to the best solution.

"Agreed," I answered. "We have already reached a diplomatic agreement with the Union of Terran Inhabitants. I think the matter should not be too complicated. Do any of you have suggestions?" I raised my eyebrows and scanned the room, tensing my muscles while I braced for impact.

"If I may interject, Your Highness," Lifiya said, "It may clarify your plans to know that the scanners do have a significant range."

"How significant?" I asked with intrigue.

She looked to her assistant, who meekly added, "Based upon the density of specimens in the environment, the range of accurate detection can fluctuate some, but approximate range is between 100 and 300 parcils, Your Highness."

"Not bad." I nodded. I was impressed with the measurements. A device so significant needed to be as precise and advanced as possible.

Akrawn, who had kept quiet until now, finally joined in. "I have been informed that excitement among the human females has begun to grow at the prospect of marriage to Trilyn Royalty."

He folded his pale hands in front of him, coal-black hair falling around the harsh angles of his face. "Our society is wealthier, infinitely more technologically advanced, and we have none of the issues of political instability or resource mismanagement they do here on Earth. I say we have the upper hand. We should use it. Let them come to us. A contained space will also make detection easier."

Manzar grunted. "There is sense in this. We make

ourselves vulnerable by going out and moving through their world. Far safer for us to conduct this search on our own territory."

Lortnam scratched the olive skin of his chin as he thought. "It needs to be done in an orderly, controlled fashion then. We can host a forum at a set time and announce it with an open invitation?" His voice showed enthusiasm.

Rawklix yawned. "A forum? Could we make the mating process any more methodical or dry? Let us throw a party, at least. If we must chain ourselves to some random human, why shouldn't we have a good time in the process?" He smirked with youthful arrogance.

For once, I agreed with my pleasure-seeking youngest brother. "Rawklix, though tactless, makes a good point. There is no reason we cannot enjoy ourselves. Besides, making the occasion festive may ensure a greater number of attendees, which will improve our chance of success."

Agreement was murmured, and plans began to take shape. Finally, we were getting somewhere. I loved to see unity come together. Brainstorming held an important place in this palace.

I thanked Lifiya and her assistant and dismissed them

to resume their work. After collecting samples from myself and each of my brothers, they rushed off to finish the devices. They hurried away with chattering and bubbly enthusiasm. At least they were engrossed in their work and loved to produce something that would reach the masses and change the world we lived in.

An hour later, the matter was settled. We would host a gathering at the week's end, here on my ship, which functioned as a remote Central Palace. Depending on how successful the occasion turned out, we would do the same at each of my brother's ships. We were aiming for the highest numbers possible, and we had to make the first event engaging, enticing, and thrillingly entertaining.

"We'll want to contract more human staffers beyond the few who have already been employed," Lortnam added. "This event should conform to Earth culture wherever possible and be as close to their traditional gatherings as we can make it."

Rawklix closed his eyes. "Please let that include orgies! Please let that include orgies!" His lips curled into a mischievous grin.

"Pardon me, Your Highness." Coel cleared his throat. "But we've surpassed the allotted time for today's council." He was right, I realized. The concentration of us all being here on one ship made us all vulnerable. As the future rulers of our planet, we did not have the luxury of taking such things for granted.

I nodded professionally. "Thank you." I turned back to my brothers. "We will conduct remote conferences for the preparations." I gave them each a glance, locking eyes with them to ensure they understood the protocol and plans to take off from here.

Each of my brothers excused themselves from the council room, making their way to their own itinerant pods that would return them to their individual vessels. One by one, they disembarked, and I was left alone in the great council room with my own thoughts. My head screamed with ideas, fantasies, and hope for the future. There was no shutting off my emotions. I was always going to be spinning in the web of my own making.

I shared Rawklix's concerns about being linked to a female I would not otherwise have chosen for myself, of course, but what good did it do to give space to such worry in my mind? There was, after all, nothing to be done about it. I was born into a position of the highest privilege, and along with it came the weight of duty. I would not shirk it now, when my service mattered most. Cosmetic and surface beauty were always fixable. Saving my species was of the upmost importance now.

The idea of returning to Trilyn appealed to me, as well. As the future High King, my successful return would do a great deal toward restoring stability to our kingdom. Indeed, though I may never fully silence the fears at the periphery of my mind, I felt quite pleased at the prospect of fulfilling my duty to my people and ensuring the survival of our race. Surely, there could be no greater honor.

I walked down the great hall with its transparent floor, allowing me an unimpeded view of the Earth metropolis below. We hovered in the atmosphere above what was called New York, I was told. Though I longed to set foot once more on Trilynian soil, there was a certain beauty to the glitter of lights that spread across the land, twinkling like burning embers.

The lights from the city below twinkled like tiny stars. The energy was electric and was already rubbing off on me. My heart raced as I stared down at the earth below. Was my future mate somewhere down there? Would we fall in love easily? So many unanswered questions lingered, begging to be answered.

The artificial lights would fade soon as the planet's rotation caused the city to be bathed in the life-giving rays of Earth's sun. Somewhere, down below in the sparkling ether of the night, was the woman whom I would wed and share my life with. For a moment, I let myself feel the warmth of hope. If I embarked on this adventure with an open mind and a positive attitude, I was bound to succeed.

CHAPTER 2

AMY

"Tell me something, Amy," Darla said, her lean frame silhouetted in the wide doorway of the dark kitchen where I'd been working all day.

I looked up, the sick feeling of dread coiling in my stomach as I asked, "Yes, Darla?" I swallowed hard and willed myself not to allow any of my fears or trepidation to escape.

"How is it that you are so incompetent? Do you think you were just born a simpleton, or was it growing up as gutter skuzz that did it?" I looked down, avoiding her catty grey eyes and willing myself to be numb and remain silent. If I didn't respond to the jabs, then I hoped this encounter wouldn't last as long.

The other kitchen workers had the good sense to scurry away from the central prepping table I was working at, anticipating Darla's tirade. If she was in the kitchens, it was to chew on someone. Luckily for the other workers, we all knew I was her preferred victim. I could hardly blame them for withdrawing, though just once, it would be nice to go a day without her abuse. I didn't expect anyone to stick up for me, but it was just as well. I didn't want to hold onto false hope.

Darla came forward, surveying the racks of delicate pastries and confections I'd been frantically churning out as quickly as I was physically able. She grabbed a plaited brioche, still warm from the oven, inspecting it. She scrutinized the treat as if she were just ready to pounce on any microscopic flaw. It seemed silly that she bothered with the pretense. We both knew it wouldn't meet her standards, no matter how perfectly prepared the item was.

"By now, I should know better than to expect anything else," she said, tossing the fluffy, buttery brioche in the waste shoot along with the rest of the tray. My heart dropped through my shoe at her hateful gesture, but I didn't flinch. "Since your dim-witted goldfish brain is incapable of holding onto information for more than a few minutes, let me remind you that we are preparing a feast for royalty.

Royalty! Do you understand what that means? That means that this has to be *flawless!*" Her voice carried through the room like a siren screeching through the night.

She knocked over several more trays, the metal clattering in a deafening clamor. "This is all shit!"

I held my breath and waited for her tantrum to end, if it ever would. Sometimes, it was better to ride out the storm than to avoid it.

My knuckles turned white as I forcefully kneaded the massive mound of dough, refusing to give in to the anger bubbling inside me. In the refugee camp, on the streets, I'd done what I had to survive, things that in a perfect world, I'd maybe regret. But violence wasn't something I got to shy away from. Life isn't sunshine and peaches for a homeless teenage girl with a baby. Hard times were a way of life for me.

It was different now, though. I had something to lose. I was on the way to getting Corinne and me out of that and into a better life, and the instincts that kept me alive before had no place here. I had to bite my tongue until I tasted the bitter, coppery taste of blood in order to prevent myself from spewing vile words at this terrible woman in front of me.

"You know what gets at me?" Darla said, coming up

behind me, oblivious to the well of anger inside me. "I gave you every opportunity, took you out of the gutter, took you under my wing, and this is how you repay me? This is the most important event we've hosted. If it doesn't go off perfectly, it reflects on *me*!" She yelled dramatically and waved her hands in the air as if she were swimming against the swell of a panic attack. "And isn't it just my luck that I have little bitches like you down here, sabotaging everything I've worked so hard for! What is that wretched smell?" She turned toward the saucier and scowled. Her nose wrinkled with patronizing disapproval.

He was a bow-legged man with a deep scar that extended from his hairline to his chin. He'd seen his share of horror. All of us had our scars, though. Some were just better hidden than others. Mine were tucked away beneath the surface and I never wanted them to see the light of day.

She marched around the room, laying into the other staff members who were unfortunate enough to still be stuck at their stations, and I let my mind wander, letting go of my anger in favor of better thoughts. You learn little tricks like that as a refugee. When things get too rough, too hard to process, you shut it out. Little tactics for preserving your sanity. It was a survival instinct of sorts, and I did what I could in order to not implode on myself.

I felt sorry for the ones currently receiving the brunt of her fury, but I'd endured my fair share in the process along the way. I blocked Darla's shrill screeching out and let my thoughts drift to that secret place in my mind. The place I escaped to with *him*. In reality, my existence wasn't even a speck on Prince Gardax's radar, but in my mind, he was *mine*.

And in my mind, he made me his. Just the way I wanted it to be. The private seclusion of my mind was my oasis in a desert of chaos.

If I closed my eyes, I could almost feel the warmth of his skin, pretend that he was holding me to him. He was the most beautiful man I had ever seen, and he wasn't even a man—not a human one, anyway. It didn't matter, though, because he made me feel more like a woman than I had ever felt. Shivers and trembles of pleasure ran up and down my spine. There was no euphoria that could ever match the depth of passion that I felt toward him.

He would kiss me gently, drawing all the stress and aches from my body as he murmured softly, assuring me that I was safe, that Corinne would be safe, that everything was going to get better. His hands were so strong as they stroked my back, my shoulders, massaging my tired muscles . . . not that princes probably gave massages, but it was my fantasy, so why not? There were no rules in the cobwebs of my lust-clouded mind.

It would have been the ultimate humiliation if anyone knew what went through my mind in moments like that. The heat of desire and shame flushed my cheeks and sprinkled them a rosy red color.

How ridiculous that I, a lowly, pathetic cook and maid, dreamed of Prince Gardax's lips curving in a secret smile meant just for me. It was pitiful, no doubt, but when you live most of your life in either a warzone or a refugee camp, you don't exactly have a lot of happy memories to pull from.

So naturally, I created my own pleasurable world where I was in charge of my fate and blissful serenity accompanied me from all sides. I created little stories in my mind, dreamy, romantic scenes that were about as far removed from reality as I could get. It helped me get through the grueling, insufferable days. I tried not to stay locked in the daydreams for long. I reserved those times mainly for sleep or when Darla was yelling at me and everyone else in her tornadic path.

Sometimes, when I was there well before dawn, baking pastries for his breakfast in the dark, warm kitchens, I'd imagine him coming in, taking the rolling pin out of my hands, and carrying me to his private chamber. Maybe we'd curl up together and talk for hours or maybe we'd sleep. Maybe we would do a combination of both. I yearned for the touch of another. I craved conversation and someone who would be interested in me and would want to get to know me.

Was it sad that my fantasies with a gorgeous alien prince involved sleep? Definitely, but when you only get an average of four to five hours of sleep a night, that deprivation seeps into everything. Of course, there were plenty of daydreams where we did more than sleep.

Whatever we did, it was far, far away from this awful, crowded, heated room. I'd never seen the private wing of his ship, if 'ship' was even the right term for it, but anything had to be better than the sweltering kitchens. It was like a sweat lodge in here, and I was layered in chef's clothing that didn't do my perspiration any favors. I wanted to sweat in other ways. Other ways that involved Gardax.

Cloaked as the structure was with stealth technology, all but the main hull was invisible from the exterior. From the ground, it was almost imperceptible, just a small aircraft among the clouds. But if the chatter among the staff was to be believed, there was much,

much more to it. The shuttle that carried us to work dropped us at the service port and we exchanged stories of the glimpses we caught.

Few knew how large the place really was, and I certainly was never given leave to go exploring, but it sounded massive, a maze of finely furnished chambers and passages that I would have loved to wander. In my deepest fantasies, I'd be waltzing through those doors with elegance and grace, adorned with the finest jewelry that money could buy. I wasn't materialistic in reality, but like I said before, a girl can dream.

I'd only seen the prince a few times. There was my first day, when I came to work with a group of new recruits aboard his vessel, two months prior. It was brief, and I was so nervous I'm not sure I remembered to breathe. That whole time was a bit of a fuzzy blur in my mind. I naturally blocked out trauma in my life.

He was the first alien I'd ever seen. Before the Trilyns arrived seeking a treaty, the only other alien life-forms humans had encountered were little more than single-celled organisms on one of Jupiter's moons. It was utterly shocking to discover that there was a sentient, intelligent, and frankly, gorgeous race out there. I wasn't ever afraid of them, especially if they were here seeking peace and unity. I was more infatu-ated and curious of them than anything.

Aside from being incredibly tall, with muscles carved so finely he might have been a statue and eyes the exact shade of the freshly ripened corn that covered the plains of the home I was forced to flee, he looked like any other inordinately stunning human. I'd heard whispers that they were trained warriors as well, despite their royal upbringing, and it didn't surprise me. The way he moved was so controlled, so power-ful. His physique was mesmerizing, intoxicating.

There had been a handful of times I'd passed him in the main hall, but he hadn't seen me. He was always speaking to someone or occupied in some way, always distracted, always serious. I had imagined royalty—alien or otherwise—led lives of luxury and relaxation, but I had yet to see Prince Gardax in any state of ease. I wondered if he took his own mental vacations, if he checked out and ran away to some happy place in his mind . . . and if he did, what sort of things he daydreamed about. I knew that he had to keep his air of confidence and leadership. He had a lot on his plate, as I could imagine.

Then there was the day he gathered the human staff aboard the ship to inform us of the impending party. His piercing yellow eyes had passed over me as he spoke, surveying the crew. It was completely idiotic, but my nerves had a field day as I sat there listening to his deep, commanding voice, hoping he'd notice me. I didn't know how I could stand out from the crowd to draw his attention, but I wanted his eyes, those piercing eyes to land on me and lock.

Then again, I thought as I looked down at my dingy apron, a wisp of flour-coated hair fluttering into my eyes, there wasn't much to notice, especially when Prince Gardax could literally take his pick of women. I'm sure I wasn't even on his radar. He was a prince, after all, and probably had women all over him.

Everyone knew why the princes had come. Their planet had been overtaken by some kind of virus that had rendered their females infertile. To ensure the continuation of their species, the princes had been sent to find human brides, and there was definitely no shortage of beautiful women who were dying to volunteer for the position . . . women I could never compete with. I was ordinary, a refugee who would never stick out.

What was I? I had nothing to recommend me. I was little more than an underfed refugee living in Union housing with no advanced education and no prospects beyond domestic work. I would never hold his interest in my condition or situation.

I sighed and refocused my attention on the sound of Darla's voice getting closer to me again. My muscles immediately tensed up, bracing for impact of the plume of anger she always had, ready to lash out.

"Do any of you have even the faintest concept of how big of a deal this is? Apparently not, or else I wouldn't be looking at a bunch of slack-jawed ingrates doing the bare minimum! We're behind schedule, and unless you want to work through the night, I suggest you all start picking up the pace!" She tossed another tray on the floor.

For someone who claimed to be concerned about completing our tasks on time, she had a funny way of showing it. Time was wasting while we all stood there, fearfully cowering under her command. We could be spending the time being productive, but she was throwing our supplies all over the room. It was a wonder that she didn't get a sore throat from all the screaming and yelling she liked to do.

"These racks are supposed to be half-full already." She motioned to the line of preservation racks that would keep the food in stasis until it was laid out for the hundreds of anticipated guests. "Look at this! This is pathetic! If the party wasn't in three days, I would fire the lot of you!" The veins in her neck bulged in protest.

"We're all working as hard as we can, Darla," I ventured, unable to bite back the comment. It had dripped from my tongue before I had a chance to convince myself not to do it. I couldn't afford to lose this job. Employment was too scarce and I had more than just myself to look out for.

"Oh? Oh, really? Well, then why is it I got a request from you to take tomorrow night off?" She sneered down at me, an evil glint in her eye. She stared at me as if she despised me and wanted to squash me like a bug under her shoe.

I looked up, surprised. She had already told me I could have the night off. My heart dropped with disappointment.

"It's Corinne's birthday—" I started, but she cackled in that creepy, brittle voice of hers as if my personal affairs were none of her concern and she couldn't care less about them.

"So, the little sponger is having a birthday? Well, wouldn't it be a nice present for her to have a big sister who doesn't just expect handouts? You're not going anywhere." She spun, eyeing the other prep workers and cooks. "Any of you! Don't think I won't be coming back before your shifts are over to see what you've got to show for yourselves . . . and if I'm not happy with what I find, no one is going anywhere."

She stomped out of the kitchen, and for a beat, we all held our breath, waiting to hear her if she'd come back before the collective sigh was released. I stared at the ceiling so the well of hot tears wouldn't instantly pour down my face like a broken-hearted waterfall.

"What a pain in the ass." Felix, one of the grill cooks, grumbled and kicked the side of a table with resentful scorn.

Quiet murmurs of agreement were shared, but I kept quiet. If I'd learned anything from all the years on my own, it's not to trust anyone. I couldn't be certain if any one of them might turn on me. Keep your friends close, but your enemies closer. In this day and age, I had little time to make either.

Of course, I wanted to defend myself against Darla's rants. And sure, I'd like to vent with everyone else about pulling fourteen-hour days of grueling work in the stifling heat of the kitchens in this floating alien palace. But I also need to survive. So, I bit my lip, swallowed my frustration, and kept my head down. There was no room for error or protest. I had to think of Corinne above all else. Her wellbeing was front and center in my mind.

When I first got hired on the ship, I'd been foolish. I'd thought I could trust people, thought that this was my magic ticket to a better life for Corinne and me. Darla had been so friendly at first. Looking back, it was clear that she was looking for weakness to manipulate. She was nothing if not crafty. Darla knew exactly how to put pressure on people, how to bully them, how to get under their skin and make them feel like the tiniest scrap of human existence. She also knew how to extract information.

She was a snake in the grass, ready to pounce. She was a wolf in sheep's clothing, or any other common phrase used to describe people like her. Well-meaning as my coworkers might have been, I didn't trust any of them not to repeat my complaints to her to save their own skin. It just wasn't worth the risk.

I could almost laugh, looking back at how misguided and naïve my first impressions of her had been. She'd seemed so genuinely interested in being friends, checking in with me through training, even coming over to our apartment and meeting Corinne. The reversal had slapped any foolish notions of friendship clean out of my mind though. It was as if Darla had flipped a switch and completely altered her demeanor in a flash.

You'd think it wouldn't have surprised me so much.

After narrowly escaping a violent, bloody war that claimed my parents and scrounging to survive as a thirteen-year-old taking care of her baby sister, there shouldn't be much optimism left in me. I've seen enough backstabbing, enough betrayal, enough violence to last ten lifetimes. Maybe I was just too tired, too relieved at the idea of someone looking out for me for once, that I didn't want to see it.

Either way, Darla reminded me of the truth. No one would ever have my back, no one except Corinne, and for Corinne, I had to endure. There was no other option. We were family, and we had to preserve that tie at any and all cost. I'd do anything to keep Corinne under the umbrella and blanket of my security.

I started plaiting the dough for another tray of brioche and let my thoughts drift back to that happy place, the place that didn't have to be tainted by reality. My hands were shaking with anger and anxiety, but after a few minutes, I began to plateau and calm down.

I wondered what Prince Gardax would look like at the party, whether he'd eat the cakes and tarts I'd made while dreaming of him . . . if he'd find his bride. Envy lashed at me like a whip, but it was no use in dreaming that he'd ever be mine.

With a sad smile, I let myself imagine what it would be like to be one of the guests, to have his eyes upon me, to be the focus of his attention. The sigh that escaped was entirely involuntary, but I was fully immersed in my own little world while I worked.

"Contents of bay four have surpassed maximum preparation cook time," the automated voice announced.

Sure enough, the distinctive smell of charred dough filled the space. I rushed forward and sent up a silent plea that Darla wouldn't smell the burned fumes and come charging back into the kitchens.

I pulled the pan out and singed my wrist in the process, a painful reminder to get my head out of the clouds and back to reality. I lived to dream but dreamed to live.

CHAPTER 3

GARDAX

I adjusted the short, stiff collar of my jacket and surveyed myself in the reflective panel outside the ballroom. The smoky sound of a human singer's voice sounded faintly through the walls, and I took a deep breath, preparing myself.

"Ready to find your bride?" Darbnix's heavy hand landed on my shoulder. He squeezed and gave me a bittersweet smile.

I glanced at my brother's reflection beside mine. We were both dressed in human formalwear, groomed and readied to meet our destinies. If Darbnix felt nervous, it didn't show, and I envied his eternal calm. Nothing ever seemed to bother him and issues rarely set him off.

"Readier than Rawklix, I suppose," I joked. My laughter sounded far away and foreign.

Darbnix chuckled but shook his head. "He's already in there, and I'm sure he's had his share of Tora pollen to take the edge off."

I nodded. "No doubt. Well, let's get this over with then," I added and pulled out my scanner. The device glowed with a dull light.

We walked together in silence to the plain black wall, and as we approached, the whole of it dematerialized in an instant, granting us entrance before reforming behind us. We didn't even feel a thing during the transition.

"Their Royal Highnesses, Prince Gardax of Erebis and Prince Darbnix of Noor," the melodic artificial voice of the ship's internal information system announced, naming our governing territories despite the fact that our human guests had no knowledge of Trilyn geography and were probably confused.

Suddenly, we were faced with a mass of humans, most of them women. The sheer volume of femininity was overwhelming, and the air hung humid with it. The scents of various types of perfume stung my nostrils. It was an estrogen party for us to feast upon.

"How is that thing supposed to pick up on just *one*

woman?" Darbnix pointed to the gadget and eyed me skeptically.

"Honestly, I guess we will just have to find out. Your guess is as good as mine." I scanned the room with intrigue and curiosity.

Bright, sparkling fabrics shimmered around us as we moved through the warmly-lit, crowded room. Seductive, hungry smiles flashed, and while I was the one hunting for a wife, the way these women watched us felt faintly predatory. The thought that they would happily devour me crossed my mind more than once.

We were being eyed as if we were prime real estate. The prospect of being a piece of meat for these women both rattled me and shook up my senses with wild delight.

It was mildly intoxicating, somewhat thrilling, but mostly suffocating. The eager expressions in these women's eyes told me I could have any of them, all of them, even. They weren't even trying to hide their desperation, which was slightly peculiar.

While I waited for my scanner to give me a signal, I allowed myself to mingle and socialize. There was no point in just standing there. I might as well be productive during this venture.

"Prince Gardax, you know how to throw a party," a

lone male guest said. He was tall, with dark skin and silver-streaked black hair. He seemed familiar, and soon enough, I placed his face. He was on the Union's Ruling Committee, one of the politicians with whom we had negotiated. He threw me an enthusiastic grin.

"Thank you. My brothers and I are grateful for your attendance and pleased you are enjoying yourself." I inclined my head with a swift bow.

"I assure you, the gratitude is mutual. I'm very eager to get to working with your scientists," he said, referring to the conditions of our alliance. In return for allowing our presence and for some assistance in our pursuit of human brides, we had agreed to share with the Union some of Trilynia's space-fold technology. We were always looking for a way to join forces for a common interest. It was always better to gather intergalactic allies than enemies.

Having observed the state of their society, it became clear that these humans were quickly outgrowing their home planet. Sharing with them our knowledge of shipcraft and interstellar travel was a small concession to ensure the continuation of my people and likely, through time, the fate of their own species.

"And we will be pleased to share what we know with your academics. But surely, tonight is not for work.

Please enjoy the refreshments and entertainment," I urged him.

I gestured around to the lavish array of food spread out on tables and cocktails of just about every concoction as the dull hum of conversation could be heard as people mingled.

"Indeed, I don't want to keep you from your many lovely guests." He smiled suggestively and raised his glass. "In fact, I fear for my safety if I monopolize any more of your time. Happy hunting, Your Highness!" He let out a high shriek of exuberance.

As soon as he turned and headed away, a rush of women crowded the space he had vacated, like a vacuum. They were swarming me from all angles.

"Your highness," a woman in a sheer dress that, while it covered her from neck to toe, left almost nothing to the imagination, said, curtsying before me. Her soft black curls reached her waist, and she licked her lips as she let her gaze travel over me. "Please allow me to submit myself," she said, running a hand along the line of her waist and hip, "for your appraisal." Her ocean-blue eyes left a current of electricity charging through the air.

"My lady," I said, bowing over her hand with a flourish in the Trilyn fashion. I watched as she swooned by batting her eyelashes and grinned eagerly from my direct attention given to her.

Unfortunately for her, my scanner didn't emit even the faintest beep. "Alas, we are not a match, madam." I hated to rain on her parade, but the truth spoke for itself. I was a ruler, not one to waste time on evasively leading anyone on.

Her expression and shoulders slumped for just a moment before she slinked closer and persisted. "With all due respect, are you going to trust that hunk of metal or your own instincts?" she asked in a breathy whisper. "I promise I'm very eager . . . to please." She licked her lips and continued to fawn over me, making movements to reveal her cleavage and bare her thigh.

I stepped back, smiling diplomatically. "And any other gentleman who engages your company is very lucky for that, but sadly, I cannot be him." I had to let her down easy, but there was a twinge of formality and firmness laced in my voice.

She shrugged, and the half-smile that touched her face looked infinitely more natural. "Well, can't blame a girl for trying! Nice place you've got, by the way." She was making small talk, hesitating like a child who had been told to go to bed but who wanted to stall as long as they possibly could get away with.

Pushed aside by other women eager to be scanned, she hurried off to offer herself to one of my brothers. There was always another prince lurking about that she could hunt down and pounce on. I wished her all the best.

And so it went for what felt like an eternity. Women presenting themselves, some more aggressively than others, but none of them elicited a reaction from my scanner. It was hard not to feel disappointed. I did not expect instant success, but not only was my scanner silent, but I was likewise personally unmoved by the women before me. It was foolish to hold onto any romantic notions, but part of me still hoped that I'd know my match when I met her, without the aid of some lab-created instrument.

There even was a part of me that secretly wondered if my scanner was working properly. Its buttons were on as if it were properly functioning, but I wasn't getting a signal on any of these girls. Surely, one of them was a match?

Unfortunately, I was not bowled over by any such sensation as I moved through the party, interacting with our guests. If anything, I felt a bit jaded by the whole affair. It was a bit daunting to put myself on the line like that and expect immediate results without any effort being put in whatsoever. As a prince, I was used to receiving a sizable amount of attention, but by tonight's standards, it fell under an entirely different category.

All these women throwing themselves at myself, at my brothers. None of them knew us, knew anything of the role they hoped to win for themselves. They saw only the grandeur of our affair, the fine clothes, the sleek technology of my ship. Their motivation was superficial, and I wanted more. Yet, I needed someone ready to dive right into this life.

I yearned for someone who would be willing to play both roles. I wanted a mate who would love me for me, not all the flashy and expensive things I owned. I also needed a strong woman who possessed the capabilities of portraying leadership roles of her own.

I shook my head, trying to push away the conflicting interests in my mind and focus on what must be done. There were plenty of grazing breasts and 'accidental' collisions, and I nearly laughed at the brazenness of our human guests, though none of it moved me.

I was waiting for that spark, that connection. I was ready to be mystified by my soulmate. I expected her to take my breath away the instant our eyes locked. It was a ridiculous assumption, no matter how hopeful I was.

Across the room, I saw Rawklix dancing with a buxom woman whose hair was the same shade of pale gold as his. The glazed, flushed look on his face told me Darbnix's guess about Rawklix's intoxication was spot-on. I shook my head. The pollen of the Tora flower that grew so plentifully in Rawklix's territory was the most potent and truest aphrodisiac known, and Rawklix was quite fond of indulging in it. I shook my head and rubbed my temples with frustration. Rawklix was clearly not seeing the whole point of this entire shindig tonight.

Surveying the room, it seemed my youngest brother was not the only one caught up in the sensual attention. Jinurak and Lortnam were together, a crowd of women cooing over them. Being identical twins was always an easy novelty for them to exploit. Even under normal circumstances, attention flocked to them because they were different.

Akrawn wore his share of jewels, a testament to the riches of the continent he ruled, gaining him his own crowd of admirers, and Darbnix was showing his watch lizards off to a number of wide-eyed guests, letting them pet the tiny creatures. Manzar moved through the crowd with focus, scanning and denying any attempts to further engage his attention. *At least one of us is on task*, I thought. I gave Manzar a subtle nod of approval as our eyes met across the room.

It was strange that I should feel so detached from the festivities. Erebis, the territory I governed on Trilynia, was the cultural center of our planet. I had hosted my share of parties, had enjoyed my share of women and moments of hedonism. Social events were common in my territory, and I was certainly in my element of familiarity.

Unfortunately, I was zoning out, and I didn't know whether it had to do with the artificial reason for the party or the fact that my scanner wasn't picking my mate from the crowd.

But everything was different now. I was no longer a prince at leisure to occupy himself with shallow diversions. A crisis brewed at home and I had a responsibility to fulfill. The situation was grave, and each valuable day became more important than the next. Knowing the seriousness of what lay before me, I no longer craved the same sort of youthful debauchery. I just wanted something . . . *real*.

Guests trickled in and out of the room, moving between the ballroom and the dining room where long tables had been dressed with extravagant floral arrangements and fine china. The party was fit for royalty, yet I craved something more tangible.

The décor, the furnishings, the entertainment had all been suggested by our human staff. It was a lavish, pleasant affair. If only I could summon the spirit to appreciate it. I considered wading into the dining area, but on a whim, I darted out a side entrance instead. I knew the humans had worked hard to impress me and my brothers, but I felt numb to the entire event.

My head ached, the result of having spent too long in a haze of perfume, so I went out to the main hall, hoping to find some clean air and a moment of silence before I went once more into the crush. I aimed for a few moments of peace and quiet to collect my thoughts and regroup.

The hall was empty, and I took several deep breaths, enjoying the relative silence. It was like a snake pit inside that ballroom, and I was the one being hunted.

But it didn't last long. My long-welcomed silence was disrupted.

The scanner in my pocket vibrated against my hip for a moment. I pulled it out and tapped at the glass screen. Then it shook again. It startled me because I hadn't been expecting it to start buzzing, and I was under the impression that I was seemingly alone.

I looked up, expecting to see someone behind me, fear and excitement mixing in my chest. But there was no one. I walked toward the ballroom and waited, but nothing happened. The hair prickled on the back of my neck. My senses were at peak alert. My heart pounded in my chest. Who was out there, making this device go crazy?

Confused, I walked further down the hall again. The space narrowed, and the scanner vibrated at shorter and shorter intervals. Lifiya had said the whole thing would light up and the screen would display a report when an ideal candidate was located.

A line of servants passed me with trays to replenish the buffet, some of them females, but the device didn't light. At least I had witnessed the thing working and I could live with the reassurance that it was indeed functional.

Had a guest wandered away from the party? Apparently, the scanner really did have quite a range. If someone had slipped away discreetly, then they were clearly out of my sight range. Confusion made me feel woozy. Curiosity kept me on target.

I walked with greater speed, nearly running as I followed the signal. My worst fear was losing the signal completely. I couldn't let it burn out before discovering the source. I stopped suddenly as I faced the doorway to the kitchen. The scanner in my hand began to emit the faintest glow.

My heart raced, the blood pounding in my ears. She was here. I couldn't see her yet, but the device didn't lie. She was in there, somewhere.

I looked up. The kitchen was dark and lit by a warm purple glow that emanated from the wall of ovens and open-flame grills. There were a handful of servants gathered around a series of preservation racks, so I walked forward. No one seemed to notice me at first. They were all working in their own little element, undistracted.

The scanner grew brighter and brighter and I surveyed the group. There were a handful of women, two of them who looked to be on the better side of fifty, and one short, round man, speaking rapidly and loading their hands with trays. As I approached, another woman straightened with her back turned away from me.

She was taller than the rest of the group, with a thick red braid that hung halfway down her back. She was struggling to pull a tray out of the rack, her back toward me. My jaw tensed. Could it be her? My breath held, suspended in my lungs.

Turn around.

I tried to mentally send her a signal. If she was really the one for me, then she'd feel my heart vibrating.

Another woman in the group, a perky young blonde, looked up and saw me, her eyes going huge as she screamed, stopping me in my tracks. All movement halted, and everyone turned to gawk at me, including the woman with the red braid. I'd been officially spotted.

When her eyes met mine, I felt my pulse leap. She was beautiful and somehow vaguely familiar, and I had the strangest sensation of . . . *home*.

I was intoxicated by her stare, unable to resist the current of emotions swirling through my mind as her eyes pierced through mine with astounding sensations of euphoria.

"What in the bloody hell!" came a voice behind me, setting everyone back into a flurry of emotion. In an instant, my dazed feeling of bouncing through white, fluffy clouds evaporated.

The petite blonde squeaked an apology, and before I could move toward the group again, one of the staff managers had stepped in front of me.

"Oh! My Lord! I mean, Your Highness! I'm so sorry, Prince Gardax. I didn't know you were back here!"

"Don't trouble yourself. It's fine, Mrs.—"

"Barnaby, Your Highness. Darla Barnaby." She curtsied awkwardly, then glared back at the rest of the workers. "Show some respect for the prince!" she hissed with aggressive flair.

"Really, that's not necessary," I started but was cut off as she came toward me, waving me back toward the door. She was persistent as she batted her hand and swiped it through the air. I was frozen in place, confused by her over-the-top reaction to my being in her kitchen.

"Please, don't sully yourself in these sooty kitchens. I will see to anything you may need!" She was bony and commanding, with harsh, angular features and thin lips.

"No, it's fine, please. I just want to take a look around," I started, but she bounced in front of me. She was not going to permit me to move any further into the belly of the work going on in here.

"Is something wrong with the food, Your Highness? If you're dissatisfied with anything at all, it will be fixed immediately," she insisted, backing me further toward the door and gesturing me out. She continued to glare at the cooks as if they were bugs she wanted to stab under the bottom of her stiletto heel.

I tried to turn back around to face the group, but the manager was too close, and the scanner in my hand knocked free, cracking on the floor, the light fading almost immediately. I inhaled a sharp breath of disappointment.

"Oh!" she yelped. "Forgive me, Your Highness!" Her facial features looked wounded as if she were expecting a berating battering of wrath from me any second.

My fist clenched as I bent down to pick it up, tapping at the screen. Nothing. Fury bubbled in my veins. Frustration inhibited my strength.

Taking a deep breath and gaining hold of my frustration, I turned and focused my attention on the pushy woman before me. I gritted my teeth and did my best to contain my rising temper.

I spoke slowly, trying not to let displeasure color my words too much. It was an accident, after all. She didn't intentionally break the one device that would help me find my match. The more I thought about it, the more disgruntled I became.

"There is nothing wrong at all with the food. Every one of our guests is having a very pleasant time. Thank you, Mrs. Barnaby, for all the hard work you and your employees have done to make it a success. Now, if you will excuse me, *please*, I just wanted to get to know the staff. I assure you, if I need anything, I will let you know." I hoped that my response would be diplomatic, yet firm enough to get the point across to this bony, argumentative woman.

Turning back, the group was gone.

"Oh, but the workers have gone to set out the dessert courses, Your Highness," she said, pausing before stepping closer. "But if it's company you're seeking, I would be very happy to entertain you, Prince Gardax, if you've grown weary of the party." Her eyes searched me with desperation that she was trying to recover from.

I sighed, frustrated and not liking the suggestion in her voice. She may be able to hold an iron fist over her workers and staff, but I had little patience for pushy, bossy people, especially of the human kind.

"That's quite all right. I'll come back another time. Good evening." I spun swiftly on a heel to exit the room and head back in the direction I came from.

I left the kitchen in a few quick strides before she could argue, returning to the dining rooms and searching the crowd for servants' uniforms and the particularly pretty woman with the red braid. The rooms were simply too full, however, and among the sea of made-up, adorned, and flashy guests, I couldn't find her.

Besides, without my scanner, the evening was essentially lost and I was too tired to feign any more interest in the masses of ambitious women. Slipping from the party, I made my way back to my private chamber and made plans to acquaint myself with the staff in the coming days. In the meantime, I hoped that there would be a way to repair the device.

"So what happened when Darla came in?" Corinne asked, her blue eyes wide and full of more optimism than the situation warranted. It was crazy early, and she was perched on a chair in our tiny kitchenette, wrapped in a thick blanket while I cooked breakfast before heading to the ship to do the same for the prince.

I sighed, and the warm air made a puff of steam in the cold room. "Nothing." I shrugged, tossing the omelet I was making for her. "Darla got in his face, insisting that *she* would help him. The desserts had to get out, so the rest of us went out to the dining hall. I didn't get back to the kitchen for a while, and he was gone when I did."

"You didn't see him while you were in the party?" she

53

asked, drinking her tea. She seemed oddly curious about something that if she had been there, wouldn't have been such an interesting encounter.

"Are you kidding?" I laughed, remembering the horde. "It was insane how many people turned out. I mean, I guess I shouldn't be surprised. What woman in their right mind hasn't dreamed that she'll end up being picked by one of the princes? They're all gorgeous and tall . . . and muscular . . . and with all that luxurious, black hair . . ."

"Oh, really?" Corinne smiled. "Here I thought they all had different-colored hair."

"I just meant they're well-groomed, you know? Not like the men around here who can't be bothered to shave once in a while," I lied.

"Uh-huh," she answered, looking not at all convinced. "So, trillion-dollar question—what do you think he was doing in the kitchens?" She raised her eyebrows with looming curiosity.

"I don't know. I mean . . ." I glanced at her sideways. "Okay, if I tell you this, don't go spreading it around, got it?" I leaned closer to her with paranoia as if I were afraid that someone was secretly listening to our conversation.

A massive grin cracked her face. "Ooh! State secrets!

Sister's oath," she said, crossing her fingers in the little gesture we made up a while ago to proclaim our allegiance to each other.

"Well, so I heard one of the other maids saying that they've got some kind of scanners that are supposed to identify possible matches. I don't know, I mean, it's just gossip." I chewed my lip. "But, he was holding a funny-looking little device . . . and it was glowing."

"Holy cow, Amy!" She jumped up in her chair. "You think it was someone in the kitchen then?"

It seemed crazy, impossible even, but I had racked my brain trying to think of what else could have brought the prince down to the kitchens in the middle of his party. More importantly, his party that he threw for the express purpose of finding a wife. If he had been following the device and the signal it was emitting, the only practical answer that made sense was that the device had registered someone in the kitchens.

I ran through the kitchen workers. It might have been Jessa. She was only twenty, petite and with a sweet, chirpy personality. Her blonde hair was exactly as sunny as her personality. She'd only worked there for two weeks, so I didn't doubt that Darla would grind some of that pleasantness down over time. Could it have been her? I racked my brain, trying to remember if Jessa had even been in the room when the prince had made his little surprise appearance.

I tried to imagine Jessa with the prince and was hit with a wave of nausea. I squeezed my eyes shut to instantly eliminate that nightmare from my mind.

"That'd be so wild," Amy marveled, clearly pondering the idea as well.

I smiled. "Maybe. I don't know. It's totally ridiculous. They're *royalty*. They'll probably end up with people from the upper orders," I said, feeling a bitter pang of resentment, thinking of the lucky few in the top tiers of the Union's caste system. "I mean, that's basically all that was at the party."

I set the plate in front of Corinne and she dug in eagerly. Watching her scarf down her food in a matter of seconds squeezed my conscience with regret. I wanted to give her more, all the things I didn't have. At least she enjoyed my cooking skills and what little food I did have to offer her.

She was my little sister by birth, but our situation blurred a lot of lines and our relationship was much more complex than that. Corinne was my sister, my best friend, my only family, my ally. For a thirteen-year-old, she had a lot of hats.

It had been the two of us on our own for the last

decade since I was her age and she was a toddler. It had been terrifying, overwhelming, so much more than I knew how to deal with, but I'd learned. I had to. I got tough, we both did, and we survived.

I played many roles when it came to Corinne. Sometimes I was the mother, sometimes the sister, and sometimes, I was the friend. I even had to throw some discipline in there every now and then.

Now, even though I wasn't making upper-order kind of money, I was making more than we'd had in the past, and I hoped I could put enough of it away for her to go to school, get a degree, make something more of herself than I had. I wanted everything for her. I was willing to sacrifice my career and happiness in order to help her succeed and shine.

She finished eating her share and pushed the plate toward me, but I shook my head. "You eat it. I'll snack on something on the ship." It wasn't entirely truthful, but it wasn't a downright lie either.

She looked at me dubiously. "Yeah, boiled fish guts or something else nasty that Darla deems fit for the staff?" She raised a cynical eyebrow.

I shrugged and pushed it back. "Maybe I like boiled fish." I gave her a smirk.

She narrowed her eyes, but I could tell she was still

hungry, and she eventually relented and ate the last of it. "Well, don't eat too much. You don't want to have bad breath when the prince comes for you."

I laughed. "Yeah, right." I stood and cleaned up the dishes. The apartment had two rooms, a bathroom and everything else. It wasn't much, but I liked to keep it orderly. Mom had always said you make the most of what you have, and we were lucky to have a place at all. We'd made it out of the conflict in Denver, but only barely, and we'd had to leave everything we had behind. I appreciated Corinne's humor and needed it now more than ever.

Corinne leaned back, tightening her blanket. "Why is that so ridiculous?"

"Um, you have seen me, right?" I gestured to my tall figure and my red braid. I never fussed with my hair or bothered with makeup. I worked in a hot kitchen, and there was no one there worth impressing. My clothes were tired and shabby.

"Well, I'm not going to argue that you could benefit from an update in the wardrobe department, but at least you've got boobs," she says. "Some of us are still stuck in training bra hell. Besides, he's a prince. He could buy you a makeover!" Corinne's enthusiasm erupted in her eyes.

I laughed and shook my head at her. "Trust me, you should enjoy your pre-boobdom while it lasts."

"Agree to disagree. Now back to your prince," she insisted. She waved her finger abstractly in the air as if she were fully prepared to go into daydream mode, right here, right now.

"Oh, stop it right now. He's so not *my* prince," I said, turning away, hoping she didn't see the vibrant blush staining my cheeks, courtesy of my red-head coloring which meant I could never be embarrassed without everyone knowing it.

"He could be, though. Imagine! You could pop out babies for him at rabbit-like speeds and I could lounge in the lap of luxury, your doting sister, surrounded by jewels, servants, and plates of weird alien food everywhere!"

I laughed. "Hmm. Some exchange." Now she was getting over the top with her vibrant and wildly vivid imagination.

"Okay, fine, I'll share some of the food with you." She paused then sobered. "No, but really, Amy, who knows? You should at least try and talk to him. I mean, you work *in* his house. How hard can it be?"

I rolled my eyes. "You don't know what Darla's like. Besides, I have no reason to interact with him, and even if I somehow managed that, what would I even say?" I shook my head, imagining all sorts of awkward fumbles and the accompanying humiliation. It was not a situation that I envisioned in the private seclusion of my mind.

For a moment, I didn't realize the room had gone quiet. I was too lost in my own thoughts. I finally looked over at Corinne, only to find her slumped over, palm on her forehead. My heart dropped through my feet.

Rushing over, I rubbed her back. "Hey, what's wrong? Talk to me," I whispered consolingly in her ear. It was a technique that often worked whenever she became distressed about something.

She scrunched her face, light brown hair spilling around it like curtains closing her off from me. "It's fine, just a headache."

I paused, that awful churning feeling in my gut. "Have you been having the dreams again?" I hated to bring up the touchy subject, but it was my job to protect her.

Breathing deeply, she winced. She didn't open her eyes, just nodded.

Damn it.

"We'll take you to the health bureau today. Maybe they can give you something," I reassured her consolingly.

She pushed me away. "No, we both know they can't. And we both know you can't miss work. I'll be fine. We can't afford for me not to be."

I hated that she was right, and the frustration boiled in my blood. But there wasn't anything I could do. She was right. If I missed work, Darla would happily fire me and then we'd end up on the streets. The health bureau wouldn't do anything. Let's face it. Darla was just itching to have grounds and a reason to kick me to the curb, leaving me out on the streets with nothing.

Every once in a while, these attacks just flared up, the effects of violence we had seen, the trauma she'd experienced as a child in a warzone. It started with nightmares, then came the racing heart that popped up at random times, stealing her breath, and finally, the migraines. It was only fitting that she'd endure an occurrence of post-traumatic stress. She'd never been officially diagnosed, but I knew the signs and the clues.

She squeezed my hand with an empathetic tug. "I'll be okay. I'll lie down for a while. Just go to work."

I was helpless and it hurt. I didn't want my conflict and torment to show in my features, but she was savvy at reading my emotions no matter how harshly I tried to cover them.

"Is there anything I can get for you? I put a little cash aside. I can get you some shortbread," I offered feebly.

Corinne opened her eyes then, just for a moment. "Talk to the prince and sweep him off his feet." She laughed weakly. Even if she was only partially kidding, her hope was pitiful and made my heart ache.

"You're impossible," I said, shaking my head before I relented. "I'll see what I can do. Now come on. Let's get you to the bed," I said, lifting her light frame up. To my surprise and relief, she yielded to my embrace and allowed me to carry her away.

A short time later, I was loaded into the small shuttle that picked up the workers for the prince's residency. I was late, but thankfully, I hadn't missed the last trip.

"Morning," Viani, an older woman who worked as a maid in the private wing, nodded. "Gonna be a fine mess to deal with today, I'm sure." She clicked her tongue and shook her head regretfully.

"Wasn't it cleaned up before the shift change?" I asked. Part of me became alarmed.

"Who knows! When I left, the princes were still out there with their 'admirers'," Viani answered with bitter air quotes.

"Sluts," the other woman, Petra, added with a cynical hiss.

Viani smirked. "Ha, you're just jealous you weren't one of them."

"Hmph!" Petra sniffed. She stared out the window and refused to make eye contact with anyone.

Viani turned back to me. "Wouldn't be surprised if they weren't still living it up, or doing who knows what else with all those randy women."

The image twisted in my stomach. I had no right to feel jealous, but it was there all the same. I would never dance among the elite, and I would never get a chance to wear a fancy, dazzling dress that sparkled when I twirled around. It was useless to dream of anything different.

"Not Prince Gardax," Petra added. "At least he had the good sense to retire early. Get away from all those artificial harlots." She nodded approvingly, and suddenly, the sun seemed to shine once more.

Viani conceded, "Yeah, well, there's gonna be a mess all the same. Must be nice to have people to do everything for you! And Tian quit last night. That means my crew is going to be short. Heaven knows how I'm going to pick up the slack."

The shuttle dinged at our arrival, and as we all stood to de-board, I couldn't blame Tian for quitting, although I felt like it was probably a rash decision that would probably be regretted later. Knowing that Prince Gardax left the party gave me a fleeting sense of hope.

"I could help," I offered quickly, remembering my promise to Corinne.

"How?" Viani asked. She glanced at me through curious eyes.

"I can run some of the trays out for lunch? I get a break after the meal goes out, so I won't be missed, and it'll give you more time to clean," I explained nervously. The plan was shady at best, but fortunately, she was too tired to question it and we parted ways a moment later.

As soon as I headed toward the kitchen, though, I began to regret it. My hand trembled already from my intensely jittering nerves and there were still several hours to go before I would even be in his proximity. I didn't know if I would fall apart before my plan even commenced.

I should probably get a grip. Really, I was just taking him a tray of food. How much could I possibly interact with him over that? Then again, I wasn't likely to have another opportunity like this. I wouldn't be on his radar, but I might capture his attention for thirty seconds. I would take what I could get.

My mouth felt dry and my cheeks flushed. The heat on my cheeks revealed to me that yet again, I was blushing.

Get a grip, Amy!

But I couldn't. Every possible humiliating scenario flashed through my mind. What if I spilled the tray? Or worse, what if I spilled the tray *and* it landed in his lap? And what on earth was I going to talk to him about? Was it even proper? What if I offended him? Would he fire me? My mind raced with worst-case scenarios that I tried to fight back with courage, but my brain was untamable.

Late as I was, I wouldn't have the chance to eat those boiled fish guts for lunch after all, but that was just fine with me. My stomach was a nervous flurry of butterflies, terror, and self-doubt, and food would have just made a crowd.

As I knocked on the door of his private quarters, tray in hand, cheeks surely flushed scarlet, I wondered if I could will myself into spontaneous combustion. Between erupting in flames or making a fool of myself in front of the prince, I wasn't sure which was worse.

I took a deep breath to pacify some of my nerves, but my hands were shaking so violently that I had to white-knuckle grip the trays in order to prevent myself from dropping them all over the floor. I wanted his attention, but not by making a fool of myself. I tried to get it together while I stood there, waiting for someone to sweep open the door.

I was engrossed in my weekly status report from my commissioners in Erebis when a knock came from the passageway. That was odd. All passages were controlled by biometric scanners that opened or closed pursuant to security clearance. While malfunctions in the onboard system occurred, it was a rarity. I wasn't expecting anyone at this time either, which befuddled me even further.

I walked over, and at my approach, the passage dematerialized to reveal a maid carrying a tray of food. In an instant, I recognized her. Her red hair was still arranged in a snug braid that rested on her shoulder. Streaks of pale blonde and cinnamon flashed in the light as she walked in, her head bowed.

"Pardon me, Your Highness. I've come to deliver your

lunch," she murmured quietly in a soft tone that was almost inaudible. I had to strain to hear her because she wasn't making eye contact.

"Yes, of course." I smiled, pleasantly surprised. There had been only a handful of women in the group in the kitchen the night before, and only she had captured my attention. She'd left a lasting impression on me without even realizing it, which made her even more mysteriously tantalizing.

I silently cursed to myself that I didn't have my scanner. Lifiya was still repairing the device after the damage it sustained. However, I wasn't going to miss out on the opportunity to acquaint myself with this beguiling creature. It was going to take some prodding, though, as she appeared far too nervous to meet my gaze. The tray rattled under her wobbly grip.

"You know the door didn't open for you because you don't have security clearance for this part of the ship, so why don't you tell me who you're really working for," I said as she set the tray beside my workstation, hoping to tease some interaction out of her.

She straightened, turning around and making eye contact for the first time. *Breathtaking.* I was awestruck, and the air froze in my lungs, briefly suspended.

"Oh, I–I'm so sorry! They were shorthanded, so I offered to help. Please, I didn't mean to break any rules!" She squirmed, her cheeks burning scarlet. She was stuttering and stumbling on her own words as she anxiously shifted her weight.

Seeing her nervous reaction, I immediately regretted the comment. "It's fine, really," I said, giving her a gentle smile. "Sorry, I was just trying to joke with you. You seem rather tense." I kept my tone even and friendly.

She gave a breathy little laugh that seemed more bewildered than amused and started pulling covers off the dishes of food. "Oh, right."

"I saw you in the kitchens, right?" I asked, hoping to put her at ease by letting her know that I remembered her, and I was also trying to engage her in a bit of lighthearted small talk.

She glanced my way so quickly I thought I imagined it, except that her eyes, the most mesmerizing hazel I'd ever seen, were too incredible for me to concoct. I was lost in her gaze, swimming in the sea of her mesmerizing current rushing around me.

"Yes, Your Highness," she demurred. She fidgeted, slightly uncomfortable.

"Just Gardax is fine, if you don't mind," I told her with a grin.

You'd think being born into royalty, I'd be used to the formal titles, but they never felt right. Maybe because it was a constant reminder that I had duties to my people that robbed me of so many of the personal freedoms others took for granted. Nobody besides my brothers and my parents could truly understand what it was like on the inside.

She laughed nervously. Her gaze flickered between me and the floor. "Uh, I don't think I'm allowed to do that."

I leaned back in my chair and surveyed her for a moment. She was beautiful in a totally refreshing way, completely distinct from the affected beauty I had been confronted with last night. Slender, tall, with skin so flawless and creamy, I had to wonder if it would taste milky-sweet as well.

There was something natural and ethereal about her beauty. She wore little makeup and wore clothes that looked as if they had seen better days, yet to me, this was more attractive than the showy women confronting me at the party.

Realizing my body was warming and reacting to her in a way that wasn't going to do me any favors just yet, I grabbed a piece of fruit off the tray and bit into it before answering, "My ship, my rules." I gave her a sly grin to let her know I was just being playful.

"So, you're using the same authority that you don't want me to acknowledge to force me to call you by your name?" she answered, a faint challenge in her tone. If she was humoring me, she held a steady poker face.

I smiled, happy she was making steady eye contact now. "You're feistier than you let on, aren't you?"

She blushed. "No, I'm just pointing out your lapse in logic." Her lips twitched in an ever-so-slight curl of amusement.

"Mmm, and I appreciate that. Not many aside from my brothers are willing to do that. Well, we've established that I'm Gardax. What may I call you?" I leaned in closer and raised my eyebrows expectantly.

She glanced behind her to where the entrance had sealed once more, as if she was afraid she would get in trouble. Biting her lip, she looked back to me. "Amy. My name is Amy Allen."

"Amy," I said, drawing the sound out. "It suits you." Indeed, it was true. Her facial features looked like an Amy.

"Does it?" she asked, smiling now. She shrugged. "I always thought it was kind of plain and ordinary."

"Nonsense," I told her, cringing that she would even view herself that way. Then I nodded. "It's a strong sound, but not hard, not abrasive. It's soft but not overly adorned, not contrived. It has a genuine, pleasantly familiar sound. I like it."

She bowed her head with a blush and raised her eyes back to mine, peering at me through her lashes. "That's a lot to take away from two syllables."

"I'm a good judge of character." I shrugged. I sat up and inspected her coy behavior.

She laughed. "And modest about it, too?" There was a playfully sardonic tone in her voice.

I smiled. "Perhaps not. But you have to be good at gauging people in my position. It pays to know who is worth trusting and who isn't. There is little I detest more than a liar. Now, you strike me as someone I can trust. Do you agree?"

She nodded. "Absolutely, but I'm nobody . . . I mean, I'm not sure why it matters since I just work in the kitchens." She absentmindedly glanced behind her as if she hadn't expected to have been here this long.

"Yes, the kitchens, precisely. Please, take a seat," I said, gesturing to an open chair in the small chamber.

She looked uncertain but did at last, to my relief. I wanted to unravel the mystery of this beautiful woman who had been hidden away in the kitchen. I wanted to discover her, pick her brain. I wanted to know everything about her.

"Are you hungry?" I asked. "Please, have some. I will not eat it all myself, I assure you." I prodded her, though she seemed reluctant and finally only relented to take a small morsel of cheese that was barely more than a nibble.

"I assume I don't need to explain why I hosted the party last night," I started in a reluctant voice.

Amy shook her head, a few stray auburn strands coming loose. "I don't think there is a conscious person on Earth who doesn't know," she said, grinning. Her eyes were stunning, electrifying. She enhanced my senses. She made me curious.

I nodded, acknowledging the celebrity that had attached to myself and my brothers. "Though our situation may seem . . . glamorous, perhaps, it's much more serious than that. My brothers and I . . . there is a lot of pressure on us to marry and marry quickly."

My voice was even more somber than I'd wanted to reveal.

She quirked a brow. "Well, I'm not sure if you've noticed, but I think you can pretty much take your pick of women."

"Be that as it may, it's more than just picking someone I like. Unfortunately, choosing someone for myself based upon my own preferences and wishes is not something I can afford to do. I have other responsibilities to my people," I said, glossing over the reproductive aspects of it. It was public knowledge already, after all, and not the most romantic of subjects. "As such, I am obliged to find the person with whom I share the greatest genetic compatibility. Fortunately, we've found a way to detect that."

She nodded. "I heard rumors about your machine for that."

"Yes, the scanner. It does not leave much room for the epic, passionate romance I had perhaps envisioned I would find when I met my future bride, but it is the most efficient means, I suppose," I said, sighing. There was no point in arguing the scanner. It was our best hope yet.

"It seems rather unfair, if you don't mind my saying. I'm sure there are good reasons for it, but I know how hard it is to have your choices taken from you, feeling like you're boxed into a corner," she said, and the somber expression on her face told me there was much more to that statement. She was hiding some private pain behind that shield of hers on the surface.

"We all do what we must to survive," I reflected, doing my best to remain gentle.

Her eyes flashed, and then she looked off, wistful. "No matter the cost to ourselves, as long as we make it to tomorrow." She looked back then, suddenly, as if she didn't mean to say as much. Our eyes caught, and for a moment, my lungs seemed to constrict in my chest.

It's her.

Surely, she must have been who the scanner was leading me to. Surely, I couldn't feel a connection like this, such a primal attraction to someone I wasn't meant for. The gates of my mind finally opened and all I saw was sunshine. All I felt was warmth.

Amy blushed again and looked away. "Well, I should probably get back to the kitchens soon." She abstractly pointed a finger skewed in the direction behind her from which she had come before.

"Right, the kitchens. Well, you might have guessed that my scanner led me there. Unfortunately, it became damaged and is being repaired as we speak. Until it's fixed, I can't know for sure who in the kitchens it was leading me to."

"Are you sure that it wasn't a mistake? I mean, shouldn't you be matched with someone from the upper class?" she asked. She sounded shocked that I would even entertain the idea that it could be someone other than a woman clothed in dazzling clothes and shimmering, expensive jewelry.

"In Trilyn society, we don't have such class separations. This means nothing to me," I assured her indifferently.

"But you have royalty," she said, her voice full of doubt. Her brow furrowed in confusion.

"Yes, but as royals, we are not considered superior in the sense that your upper classes are here. Trilyn society is much more complicated than that. Our role as royals is one more of servitude. There is privilege, certainly, but it comes at a cost, as anything does."

"I see," she said skeptically. She scratched the side of her cheek and took a deep breath.

I smiled. "I'm not sure you do, but perhaps I will have another opportunity to explain the intricacies of my culture to you." *On our wedding night, perhaps?* The thought struck me, and at any other time, it might have terrified me that I could so easily picture such a thing after so brief an acquaintance, but now all I felt was hope. I hoped I wasn't being too presumptuous.

And if there were a wedding night, there were much more engaging ways I would wish to spend it with her than explaining the history of my planet. I didn't want to bore her to sleep while I tried to seduce her at the same time.

She laughed. "Sorry, it's just hard to picture someone like *you* ending up with some lowly kitchen worker." She pointed to herself as if she had nothing to offer. It made my heart ache.

"Someone like me?" I countered. Our eyes met, and I knew she sensed the electricity, the awareness between us. My heart was beating rapidly in my chest. I had to bite back a tempting impulse to kiss her.

"Well, yeah, someone so . . . powerful and courageous," she mumbled, embarrassed, heating me with every word. "I mean, obviously, you know . . . you're attractive," she murmured as if she were humiliated to admit the words out loud or as if she would be punished severely or something.

I grinned. "Is that what you think?" My belly flipped with excitement.

"Yes—no, I mean, it's obviously a fact. But it's beside the point. That sort of thing, it just doesn't happen on this planet."

"Well, then, I suppose being from another planet has its advantages. No silly class elitism to get in the way." I smiled warmly. "From all appearances, it would appear my match has been working in my kitchens all this time. The only question is who?" I said, allowing my gaze to linger on her lips. Her tongue darted out in response, and I smiled at the involuntary reaction.

"Well, um, there are a lot of people who work in the kitchen," she responded. She eyed me with a meek and humble pair of eyes.

"True, but there were not so many in there right at the moment I came down," I argued. "You . . ." I said, dropping my tone, enjoying the rapid flutter of her eyelashes, "and a few others."

"Right. I think. To be honest, I don't remember exactly. I'm sorry." She blushed, clearly flustered.

"It's very frustrating, being so close and yet not knowing, especially when the situation is of such monumental importance to my people," I explained, rolling my wrist through the air.

She looked sympathetic then. "I can ask around, find out who else was down there at that time."

I didn't want to know who else. I just wanted to know if it was her, but I appreciated the generosity that provoked her offer and I was eager to guarantee another conversation with her.

"That's very kind of you to offer your help. I would be very grateful for it."

"I'm not quite sure what to do with a prince's gratitude." She laughed. She glanced down at her shoes.

"The options are endless," I said in a low voice, leaning forward. I was teetering on the edge of being flirtatious.

Her breathing seemed to change slightly, her eyes darkened, and right as she opened her mouth to respond, her pocket buzzed and she stood suddenly. "Forgive me, Your Highness . . . er, I mean Gardax. I really need to get back to the kitchen."

"Of course. I take it that is your supervisor," I murmured. The interruption had disappointed me.

Irritation flashed in her eyes. "Darla. She is the woman who approached you in the kitchen." She spoke with resentment that was hard to hide.

"Ah, yes." Then, just to test her reaction, I added, "So she is a potential candidate as well?"

Amy's eyes grew wide. "Oh, heavens, no! She's

married, for one thing, but she's also just . . . just terrible! Sorry," she said sheepishly. She behaved as if she wanted to vent to me but wasn't sure I would be the most trusted source for containing the burdens of her secret thoughts.

I laughed and gave her a friendly nod. "I'll make a note of it."

Getting up, I walked to the door so that the passage would open for her and made a mental note to approve her full security clearance. If she happened to wander into my private chamber again, that would be just fine with me. I was already beginning to miss our playful back and forth banter and craved to see more of her.

"It was a pleasure speaking with you, Amy. A pleasure and an enchanting surprise," I said, bowing over her hand in the traditional Trilyn way, the contact of our skin sending a thrill through me as I looked down. My gaze was surely anything but proper, but I couldn't help it.

She bit her lip and smiled. "And you . . . Gardax."

She gave me a slight bow, and I could tell that she wasn't sure how to properly bid me farewell. I found her even more adorable and attractive than when she'd first arrived in the room.

With that, she slipped out and was gone, but her smell and the sensation of her hand in mine lingered. My insides sizzled with desire that I desperately needed to satiate. I hoped to see her again. If she didn't come to me, I might eventually crack and attempt to seek her.

I wanted to chase after her, but I didn't. I needed to be patient. This was far from over. I closed my eyes and breathed deeply. I smiled at the memory of her shy smile. If anything, I was in better spirits after having that delightful conversation with her.

CHAPTER 6

AMY

The rest of my workday passed like a dream, despite Darla's best attempts to make it a nightmare. I was trying to tamp down the growing, yet preposterous, hope that I might be the person Gardax's scanner was leading him to. The idea of his choosing me made my heart flutter, but my mind was a sea of unrest. It was a ridiculous assumption to think his scanner would ever point to me.

Not that I had much experience in such things, but it felt like he'd been flirting with me. Briefly, it even felt like we'd made a connection. That kind of chemistry was hard to miss, but I was probably insane for thinking that. What would someone like him have in common with me?

Our upbringings were *literal* worlds apart, not to mention I worked for him. I just needed to shove the fanatical concept from my mind before I ended up setting myself up for disappointment.

A pleasure and an enchanting surprise.

His words echoed in my mind. Even the memory of it sent chills down my back, the way his voice had sounded, low and suggestive. The comment was innocent enough, but the look in his eyes definitely was not. It was useless trying to fight the smile that kept creeping onto my face.

"Look at you, sweet little thing. Mmm! I'll give you something to smile about, honey," some creep called out as I passed him, walking along the cracked sidewalk up to our complex.

I briefly tensed up, but it didn't last long. I'd lived in Union subsidized housing long enough to not be fazed by it anymore. I was smiling like an idiot just now, but even if I wasn't, even if I was hidden head to toe in a shapeless, unattractive parka, these lecherous lurkers would still call after me. They were desperate for any kind of attention, positive or otherwise.

"What's the matter, baby? You too good for a compliment? You lookin too good to be from the precinct.

Maybe you need someone to show you how it works 'round here." One of the lowlifes addressed me with a set of gnarly yellowing teeth.

He was following me, I realized, so I reached into the pocket of my coat and wrapped my fingers around the switchblade I always carried with me. I'd lived enough years with nothing and no one to have figured out how to defend myself, even though the prospect still terrified me, even now. Up until now, I'd been lucky enough to not have to use the switchblade, but I couldn't keep those hopes alive forever.

I didn't turn around, but I could hear his footsteps were gaining on mine. I didn't feed his predatory drive by walking faster, but my pulse leaped and I could feel the vein above my eye twitching. I began sweating under my huge parka. My survival instinct was kicking into overdrive.

The steps to the massive monolithic complex came into view, its uniform rows of sad, characterless windows lit by the throngs of people coming home from whatever meager jobs they'd scrounged up. A drifty fog floated through the air, and the dew was already beginning to saturate the grass lining the empty sidewalks.

I hurried up to the building, eager to put as many

walls and doors between myself and my admirer. But as I reached the door, a big hand slammed it closed. I gasped, startled by the event and internally cringing that I'd shown any emotion at all to my perpetrator.

I looked up at my new friend. He was an inch or two taller than me, with a wide-set frame that on a healthy man would have made him large, but he, like everyone else here in the refugee precinct, probably hadn't eaten a full meal in months. His eyes bulged out from their sockets, rimmed with a sickly red, and when his pale scruffy face broke into a smile, he put his yellowed, chipped teeth on full display.

I gulped and instinctively took a step back, careful to not tumble down the stairs leading to the building.

"Now wait just a minute, baby. Why don't you tell me what has a pretty little baby like you smiling like that? I could use a reason to smile too. Maybe you can help me with that." He reached out, putting a hand at my waist.

I didn't think, just reacted, my body moving on its own. It was eat or be eaten. I was living in a shark-infested world, and I had learned to swim years ago.

I stomped down on his foot, turning to throw an elbow into his ribs and pulling the switchblade out in one swift move, holding it against his throat. I pressed the blade against the tender skin just lightly enough not to draw blood.

"Unless you want me to carve that smile into your face, you might want to find someone else to help you out," I growled.

Putting a finger between his neck and my blade, he pushed it away as he stepped back. "Hey, now, just lookin' for some fun."

"Look elsewhere," I warned with a hissing drawl.

He nodded and staggered back. "You got it."

I turned and hurried into the building and up the five flights of stairs to our unit, stopping outside our door to regain my composure and my breath. Without the knife to protect myself with, I would have been toast.

It was stuff like this that I wanted to get Corinne away from. She was just getting to an age where she'd start attracting the same kind of notice, and it scared the hell out of me. I'd lived through enough close-calls and scraped out of enough near-misses to know how easily you could get cornered.

Corinne wasn't as seasoned on the streets as me, but I wasn't ready to go down that road yet and train her for what it was like out there in the cruel real world.

I needed to get us both out of here. The clock was

ticking. There was little time left to waste. I needed to brainstorm a plan, one that would be failsafe and protect us both.

I almost had enough money stashed away to put down a deposit on a place in Brooklyn. I just needed to keep my head down and work hard. Whatever it took, I was going to protect Corinne. She was the only one I cared about, even above myself. I never wanted to see her get hurt or have to endure the nightmares I'd faced in my life.

Of course, there was the possibility I could be Gardax's mate. I closed my eyes, retreating into fantasy. It was impossible, completely impractical, but I needed an escape. If I could even allow the private desires of my mind to flood my reality for a few minutes, maybe I could regroup and feel less rattled.

We'd chatted so easily. I loved that he didn't seem to mind when I challenged him. He was a prince, after all. He didn't have to suffer such a thing if it assaulted his vanity. He wasn't that kind of prince, though, with an ego that bruised like a peach.

I unlocked the apartment and walked in, quietly setting my bag on the small table, hoping not to wake Corinne. She was lying on her side on the sofa-bed, her small frame an almost imperceptible lump under her thin blanket. She had a compress over her eyes, a sign the migraine hadn't passed yet. Her body was a slender silhouette under the faint glow of the street-lamps scattering a dim yellow light into the room.

I set about making dinner as quietly as I could. I didn't want to make any racket that would make Corinne's migraines any worse, but I was starving. Through my rhythmic movements around the kitchen, I decided that it was in my best interest to allow myself to let my thoughts linger on Gardax.

I could almost picture our life together. The prospect made me smile. How could I even begin to adapt from barely scraping by to becoming a royal princess overnight? The idea was thrilling. Sure, I knew nothing of Trilynia or what his life was like there, but I knew if I were lucky enough to be the girl he picked, or was matched with, rather, it would be a happy life.

Not just because it would take me out of this hell-hole, but because I could tell he was kind and playful, and surprisingly, it felt like we'd both, in our own ways, gone without for the sake of others.

He had a witty, charismatic way about him, even though he wasn't native to Earth. The playful banter was able to travel the miles across the galaxy. Perhaps joy and laughter were a universal language.

We had each sacrificed something of ourselves for the betterment of the people we cared for. In the cutthroat world I'd come up in, that wasn't something I saw often. It was every man for himself.

Still, I had to remember that just because he'd flirted with me wasn't any reason to think I was the right match for him. He'd said they were looking for genetic compatibility. What did I know about that? It wasn't going to do me any good to spend too much time fixating on the possibility that I was going to get whisked off my feet by some warrior prince.

After all, the device would speak for itself. It didn't matter if we were soul mates on every possible level. If I wasn't a genetic match for him, then the dream would fade away quicker than a sunset.

"You look serious," Corinne's voice croaked.

I flinched a little at being startled, but not enough for her to notice. I glanced over to see she'd turned to face our tiny kitchenette.

I ignored the observation. "Are you feeling any better?"

"Meh." She shrugged, then yawned. "What're you making?"

I gave her an apologetic smile. "Miso and tofu. Again." At least it was food, something to eat and prevent immediate starvation.

Being the trooper that she was, or maybe just being hungry, she smiled. "Sounds perfect." She never complained, which made my guilty conscience gnaw at me even further.

I didn't tell Corinne about my conversation with the prince, especially not my promise to help sort out who else had been in the kitchens. She'd probably gouge out an eye if she found out I had offered to help him find someone else. Knowing how scrappy Corinne could be, she'd probably gouge out both of my eyes except that might hurt my chances with Gardax.

We ate what little we had, mainly in silence. I was lost in my own private thoughts, and Corinne still had her throbbing head to plague her. After that, there was nothing left to do but go to bed.

Fortunately, Corinne had forgotten about the subject for now, to my relief. I already had my own wayward hopes to contend with. I didn't need another voice in the back of my mind, skewing and altering my already confused mentality.

Despite my best attempts to stay level-headed, my heart raced when I got to work the next morning. Every time someone came into the kitchen, I looked up eagerly, hoping it might be him, hoping to see him come in, scanner in hand and walking straight toward me. I was jumpy and jittery and going through the motions of my day with a hopeful heart.

Everyone in the kitchens would surely gasp as he took me into a rapturous kiss. My lips tingled at the thought, and I smiled into the batter I was whipping. He was probably a masterful kisser. He was royalty, and his touch would probably turn my skin to gold, warming me from the inside out.

My own experience was extremely limited. The few times I'd let my guard down enough to accept a date, I'd been disappointed by the belligerent jerks I had foolishly trusted. It was just too risky. Maybe there were good guys out there, but most of them treated women like a commodity, and I couldn't afford to weed through them and take a chance that a guy really was who he seemed to be.

Not when I had Corinne to think about. I'd built up a protective wall, and it would take a jackhammer to crumble it back down again.

The thin walls of our complex couldn't hide the screaming fights of neighbors, the crashing furniture, and the awful sounds of domestic violence. There was enough ugliness around us. I didn't want to add to it. But that didn't mean I didn't dream about romance. There were stressors out there in the poverty-riddled world that were like ticking time bombs.

Our parents, despite Corinne having no memory of them, had left an impression in me of what true, unselfish love looked like. Unfortunately, the conflicts of the prior decade seemed to have destroyed any chance I might have once had at true love and all its rose-tinted implications. I was viewing the world through a cynical lens.

That is, until I got lucky enough to be recruited for Gardax's crew. I didn't often think that the universe had a purpose for me, but every now and then, I wondered whether fate had led me to places and situations on purpose.

"You look awfully damn chipper." Darla scowled and eyed me with a special kind of loathing.

I looked down, remembering that if things with

Gardax went nowhere, which I knew, in all reality, was probably the case, I still needed this job. I couldn't blow the opportunity or allow Darla to suck me into her abyss of darkness and rob me of happiness.

"Are you deaf as well as dumb now?" she barked. Her loathing meter was enhanced now. Her cheeks were stained with the red flush of anger.

I looked up at her and realized that *if* Gardax did end up matching with me, I'd one day be *her* boss. I tried but couldn't fight the glee at the thought. My lips curled into a sinister smile that I couldn't control, no matter how hard I tried to mask it.

"Is there an expression you would prefer that I wear, Darla?" I asked, knowing I was pushing my limits with her. I tried not to sound mocking but the sentence itself was daring.

"Well, isn't someone feeling awfully smart today?" she sneered. "As a matter of fact, I'd prefer that you do your work instead of daydreaming about whatever idiocy passes for thought in that shrunken brain of yours," she snarled as she continued to glare daggers through me.

Before I thought better of it, I spat back, tired of the verbal abuse. "Actually, I was just wondering what'll happen to you when Prince Gardax finds his mate."

"Excuse me?" She spun back toward me. Her eyes were red with fury.

Crap, why did I say anything? I tried to backtrack, but it was too late. I couldn't redact a statement that had already been verbalized. "It's nothing. just that."

"Spit it out or you're fired, right here, right now, you gutter trash," she growled. Her bony hands gripped her hips as if she was trying to keep herself from snapping in half with anger.

Brilliant. Now I'd stuck my foot in it. There was no way to recover from what I'd said now. I'd already said way too much.

I tried to minimize what I could, but it all came spilling out. Truth be told, I was never good at lying, but it was too late to retreat or stay silent. Once I'd opened the gates, there was no telling when I'd stop.

"The prince wanted to know who all had been in the kitchens when he came down from the party. His scanner was leading him here and he suspected that one of the kitchen workers might well be his bride."

Her eyes sparkled with an icy interest that unsettled me. She looked even more devious than usual.

"And he told you this because . . . ?" she asked as if I weren't important enough to share even more than a formal hello or goodbye with the prince.

I looked around then, realizing that everyone around us was silent, listening. Some of them were staring directly at us, arms extended in midair as they froze to watch the spectacle. Others were pretending to be busy doing other things, but it was obvious their sensors were on alert and they were fully tuned in to our heated argument.

"Well, his scanner was broken, and he recognized me from that night, so he asked me to find out who else had been down here so he could figure out which of us it might be." I smiled then, unable to restrain the dreamy tone of my voice. "Isn't it crazy to think one of us could marry him?" My eyes floated up to the ceiling. I was involuntarily allowing myself to imagine a better life out there for myself and Corinne.

Murmurs erupted around us, punctuated by gasps of excitement. I couldn't tell whether they were rooting for me or for a brawl to break out.

Darla turned around, scanning the room, her shoulders puffed out with deep breaths of anger. "What the hell do you think you're doing? Get back to work!" she shouted, then spun on her heel and rushed out of the room, taking her furious energy with her.

I thought I was surely in for some kind of retaliation for my attitude with Darla, but to my confusion, she'd completely lost interest. Not one to question a lucky turn of events, I welcomed the respite from her bullying attention. I'd dodged a bullet, at least for now.

CHAPTER 7

GARDAX

"**Y**our highness, the background checks you requested have been collected," Coel informed me as I ended a conversation with Lifiya.

"Thank you. I'll review them in my private quarters." I nodded, then turned back to Lifiya's brightly lit work station where she was bent over the device. Her brow was furrowed in concentration and a sliver of her tongue was protruding from her mouth as she worked to fix the issues.

"How soon will this be completed?" I asked with optimism.

"I'll be done repairing the screening chips today. What about your part, Inez?" she asked, looking to her assistant who sat across the room at his own station.

Inez looked up nervously, blinking his hazel eyes rapidly. "It will take me another day at least, I suspect, Your Highness." He sounded genuinely apologetic, albeit inflexible on the matter.

My jaw ticked. I was normally a patient man, but when it came to matters with the potential for so greatly impacting my life, I felt I was justified in being eager to have them resolved. I guess I should have been grateful that they could even fix the damn thing at all, but the entire ordeal was turning out to be a nuisance.

I was polite yet firm. "I will be very grateful if you are able to find any way of speeding this matter up. Now, in the interest of delaying you no further, I'll leave you to your work."

"Of course, Your Highness. I understand what is at stake. Let me assure you, we'll work on nothing else until your scanner is repaired," Lifiya said, curtsying as I left. Her tone was sincere. I trusted her to get the job done.

Despite her assurances, I felt restless. No matter how hard I tried to satisfy my eager curiosity, I couldn't stand the wait.

Finding my way back to my private quarters aboard the ship, I took the longest way possible, hoping to pass Amy somewhere along the way. It was a futile effort, however. I assumed she was at work in the kitchens, and despite my desire to go to her, I knew it would be unwise. For one, there was a chance she might not actually be whom the scanner had identified. I didn't want to expend a substantial amount of effort chasing a dead-end path.

I knew myself well enough to know I was entranced by her, and I doubted my ability to keep my attraction hidden. I didn't know the other workers in the kitchen, but I didn't want to introduce her to any undue scrutiny or make matters awkward for her, especially if it turned out that she wasn't my match. That would just lead to further problems down the road for both of us, and it wasn't worth the trouble.

Frustrated that we didn't cross paths, I entered my private training module and took out some of my energy on simulated enemies. Slicing and hammering away at my mock-attackers, I wore myself down to a manageable degree. After a while, I was exhausted and sore, both emotionally and physically.

It had always been considered imperative that, as princes, my brothers and I were trained in the arts of battle and combat. Despite Manzar's aptitude for battle strategy and his militaristic attitude, I had excelled above the others when it came to fighting ability. Being the oldest and destined as I was to be the High King, I had always borne the brunt of duty, and as such, had perhaps needed an outlet more than the rest.

Suitably exhausted, I called off the exercise and stepped into the cleansing chamber, reveling in the stinging iciness of the water as it flushed through the small space. I held my breath and squeezed my eyes shut as the water pelted me in a refreshing way.

"Vesper," I said, calling the anthropomorphized onboard computer by name, "pull up the security dossiers Coel forwarded."

"As you wish, Prince Gardax," her smooth artificial voice crooned through the speakers.

Naked but for the cloth wrapped at my waist, I spread out on my wide, plush bed, drying in the warm rush of air flowing from overhead. I inhaled a deep sigh of contentedness and allowed my body to relax and succumb to the mattress that morphed perfectly to my shape.

As I relaxed against the pillows, Vesper projected the files in front of me and I began to read, making sure to really study the words displayed before me.

Name: Jessa MacIntyre, 20

Birthplace: Municipality of Sarasota, Province of Florida, Union of Terran Inhabitants

Occupation: Prep Cook

The file was accompanied by a photo of the short blonde woman who had screamed when I came to the kitchens. She was pretty enough, petite and healthy looking. Nothing about her tempted me, though. I skimmed through her background, deciding that I should still educate myself. It felt wrong, but I forced myself to consider the possibility that each of these women stood an equal chance of being my match. I might as well familiarize myself with all of them so that I might have a certain expectation of my future.

I scanned quickly through all six files. Though Amy had promised to find out who else was in the kitchens and I was eager to speak with her again, I decided I didn't want to wait to find out who the possible candidates might be. Instead, I had Coel search security footage and identify the potential women.

When I got to the last file, my body reacted instantly. My heart pounded. My cheeks flushed with the heat of yearning. My fingertips were numb, and the rest of my body tingled and sizzled.

Name: Amy Allen, 23

Birthplace: Municipality of Omaha, Province of Nebraska, Union of Terran Inhabitants

Occupation: Boulanger/Patissier/Maid

She seemed to have a lot of responsibilities, which struck me as somewhat odd. I scanned through the previous employees, all of whom had only one assignment. Odd. Why was she the only one carrying a heftier load?

I read on, smiling when I saw her contact information. I wondered if it would be weird to reach out to her. Would that be a violation? As her employer and unfamiliar to the rules of human society, I wasn't sure.

Committing the information to memory, I turned back and started to read her history. My pulse pounded with curiosity.

Family: Parents (Roman and Julia Allen) killed in raids during Transcontinental Conflict of 2092.

So, she had been orphaned at a young age. I sympathized with her situation. My own mother had died when I was eight, while giving birth to Rawklix. The pain we shared made her even more attractive to me.

Reading further, I discovered she had assumed guardianship for her younger sister who was only three years old at the time of their parents' death. According to her application statement to the New York Provincial Refugee Board, she'd fled with her toddler sister, barely more than a child herself. The bravery and courage she must have had back then were remarkable.

Their parents had apparently been professors in some institution of higher learning but had been targeted for disseminating information about a resistance movement that would eventually win, though not before costing Amy her family and everything she had.

They were executed by a firing squad, with Amy forced to watch along with other family members of the resistance agents. I cringed at the thought of how horrible it must have been for her, unable to look away and forced to stand there and watch her parents take their last breaths.

I didn't know much about the history of these Earth conflicts, but it was clear they had left a wake of destruction. Their warfare methods, though extremely primitive and poorly calculated, were wildly and incredibly destructive. Such civilian casualties in battle would have been unthinkable to the

Trilyn, but apparently, humans tolerated this sort of indiscriminate death and violence as the just cost of war.

I couldn't help but marvel at her resiliency as I learned that Amy had managed to escape custody and smuggle herself and her sister aboard a train out of the province. The two of them had managed to scrape their way to New York, and once granted refugee status, Amy had immediately gone to work to support herself and her sister.

I took a moment to absorb this information about Amy. My respect for her was growing by the second. She had courage and she wasn't afraid to hustle against the odds. She was selfless for taking care of her younger sister in such a loving and maternal way.

Her employment was spotty and included a variety of domestic positions. From nanny to housekeeper to cook, she had adapted to whatever position she was able to earn, most of which paid next to nothing. The information didn't divulge details of how long she'd spent in each position or any reason pointing to why each job hadn't worked out.

From what I could tell, she was still supporting her younger sister. Reading through everything she'd been through, I was incredibly impressed by her strength and perseverance. Thinking back to my own brothers and how much they had annoyed me when I was thirteen, I could not imagine assuming responsibility for any of them, let alone without any support or resources.

Even as a prince, I wasn't sure if I could have been up for the challenge to mold into that fatherly and domesticated role. Amy was truly a unique individual.

She had literally raised her sister, provided for and protected her on the sheer strength of her character alone. Her sister was probably too young to even remember their parents. Amy would be all she knew and the only one who'd ever protected and cared for her. Her comments, then, about surviving no matter the cost, came back to me. My own sacrifices suddenly seemed to pale in comparison to what she'd been through, to what she still endured. Her words continued to ripple through me like an earthquake shattering the soil around me.

I returned to her picture, finding myself even more attracted to her now that I knew what she'd overcome, the resiliency of her spirit. The fact that she was not bitter or unkind struck me as well. What must she think of someone like me, who had never gone without, who'd lived in luxury, who'd never been faced with the life or death realities she encountered daily. It was humbling. Suddenly, I felt as if every complaint I'd ever uttered was just a superficial whine and I aimed to now view the world with a new set of more aware and astute eyes.

I would help her.

It was the very least I could do. I couldn't stand idly by and watch her continue to struggle just to scrape by. She and her sister must be starving with the destitute wages she earns. There must be something I could do as a Trilyn prince to come to her aid.

It struck me then. I respected her, and I wanted to use my privilege to ease her struggles. Even if she wasn't my mate, and knowing what I now did about her, I desperately hoped she was, but if she wasn't, I would find a way to improve her situation. It seemed as if she had struggled more than the rest of the women on the list. She deserved better, and I would vow to help her achieve a better life for herself and her sister.

"Sergeant Coel, Your Highness," Vesper announced, slicing through my thoughts. I had really wandered off there for a minute and had become absorbed in everything Amy.

I sat up as the passage dematerialized.

"Pardon the interruption, Your Highness, but Princes Darbnix and Rawklix have both sent messages. They wish to discuss preparations for the next gathering to be hosted," he informed me.

Of course, they were. It was rather humorous, how resistant Rawklix had been to the idea initially, until he'd seen the horde of beautiful women who turned out. He'd flipped his opinion like a light switch. I rolled my eyes and rubbed my temples. He was so frustrating sometimes. He only cooperated when it suited him.

I flexed my neck, stretching and considering. "Indeed, I suppose we should get the plans underway. One thing, Coel. I want the kitchen staff to be included in the party. See to it that we fill those positions with temporary workers or make whatever adjustments need to be done, but I want all six of the candidates there," I instructed him.

I needed to weigh my options, and having all six candidates present would help me ascertain a better idea of who my match might be, even in the absence of my device, for the time being.

"Certainly. And your brothers? Do you wish to conference with them?"

"Yes, set up the remote conference in the Council Room," I instructed him, standing to dress. I would need to talk to my brothers and discuss the details.

He nodded and left, leaving me once again in the silence of my own thoughts.

I glanced back to the picture of Amy as I pulled clothes on and wondered how long it would be before I knew. The way my skin and other parts heated at the thought of her, I wasn't sure if I could wait on Inez and Lifiya's work before I sought her out anyway. The heart often won when it came to choosing a match, and I was afraid I was heading down that same path.

CHAPTER 8

AMY

I didn't see Gardax after all, but Viani mentioned she'd had to deliver his lunch to his Council Room, some super-secret squirrel space hidden somewhere in the ship that honestly just added to the sexy aura around him.

I privately imagined meeting him in that cavelike space. I pictured it to be romantically lit. He'd strip me down to nothing, and I'd stand in front of him, naked and exposed, vulnerable and pulsing with desire.

I quickly recovered and dabbed the perspiration off my neck with one of the towels from the kitchen. I needed to snap out of these little mini-fantasies. They weren't doing me any favors and were just impulsively turning me on in a disruptive way that conflicted with reality.

Of course, the majority of the ship was a mystery to me, so for all I knew, it was a glorified washroom, but according to her, it was pretty high-tech and she'd had to go through a full body scan before being admitted to deliver his tray. I was curious and wanted to explore on my own, but I knew it would never be permitted. I'd never achieve that level of clearance.

Viani said he'd been in conversation with his brothers and upper-level staff about another party. Apparently, Gardax's brothers hadn't gotten any leads on their potential mates and so another gathering would need to be held. She hadn't been able to eavesdrop a substantial amount, but she'd heard enough of the conversation to understand what was going to happen.

I wondered how many of these we were going to host. How many billions of women were there on Earth? The idea of Darla's tyrannical attitude in the buildup to the last party put an unpleasant knot in my stomach that I tried not to dwell upon.

It was better if I didn't set myself up for anxiety before the party was even underway. I'd do my best to struggle to remain calm. I'd endured stress like this before. I could encounter it and survive again.

Then again, maybe she'd change her tune now that everyone was on high alert, knowing that one of our ranks could be his future bride. If he so much as looked in the direction of the kitchens, I was certain we'd all know right away, and I hoped the idea was enough to make Darla eke out whatever droplet of decency she had in her. If she were smart, she wouldn't want to make a scene or cause the prince to become disgruntled in any way. I had a good feeling that she'd be on her best behavior this time around.

Either way, I was terrified and exhilarated at the same time, wondering who he might end up matching with and whether it would be me. My heart pounded when I imagined the device flashing and beeping, lighting up like fireworks when he pointed it to me.

But the mind was terrible at playing tricks on a person, and as quickly as the fantasy would fade, another concept would plunge me back down to reality. I would be devastated at having to watch the scanner pick someone else instead of me. Jealousy rippled through me like a shockwave at the mere thought.

The little persistent voice of self-preservation in the back of my mind urged me to start considering other employment opportunities. I wanted to hold onto the fantasy that it would be me, but nothing was guaranteed. I knew that better than most. I wouldn't want to stick around here, being Darla's punching bag if it ended up not being me the scanner chose.

If it wasn't me, I wasn't sure I could sit by and watch as he married one of my former coworkers. It would be too much to bear. I'd already witnessed enough pain in my life. I was tired of suffering on account of the situations around me.

Maybe before we had spoken, I could have tolerated it. That was when he was more like a canvas to project my own desires onto, but now that we had met, now that I had a sense of the man behind the fantasy, well, I was beginning to suspect I might be falling in love with him.

At the very least, I was definitely well past infatuation. There was no turning back the hands of time now. We'd already broken the ice and I knew little pieces of his personality. He had been somewhat humanized to me.

On the shuttle ride home, a message came through on my phone that only fanned the flames of my growing crush. The more he engaged me in conversation, the deeper into lust I fell for him.

Have you decided against helping me?

I smiled. *No, Your Highness, but I* was *under the impression that employees aren't supposed to just wander away from their work and gossip, even if it's with their boss.*

There are exceptions to every rule, he wrote back almost instantly. My heart fluttered with every sentence from him that I read.

Warmth spread through my whole body. It seemed like an invitation, but to what, I wasn't sure. He was mischievous and secretive, a saucy trait that made him seem even more tantalizing to me.

Before I could dwell too much on what he meant, he wrote again. *I'd like to get to know you better. Starting tomorrow, you'll be reassigned to my personal staff unit, if that is acceptable to you.*

I couldn't contain my grin and wrote something horribly ineloquent like, *Okay.*

What else was I supposed to say? I didn't want to sabotage my own odds and be the reason I failed. Besides, I was still reeling in shock from the amount of attention he'd already given me thus far.

Good. Now, get some rest. I'm told I'm very difficult and unpleasant to work for. His humor and wit were apparent through his words.

Perhaps you've just had bad sources? You don't seem the domineering sort, I quipped back with a playful smile crackling through my facial features.

You'll just have to find out for yourself – Gardax. It was almost like a dare. I loved every bit of his banter.

I laughed and clutched the phone to my chest, blinking back what felt dangerously like tears. I was in trouble if I didn't yank myself out of these gleeful clouds.

Rein in the fatal attraction vibes, Amy! He's just being nice. he's probably talking to all the workers in the kitchen. I swallowed hard and tried to push the idea out of my mind that he might be sending the very same texts to other female workers in the kitchen, trying to gauge them and feel them out to see which one of us might be his match.

I'd asked around and figured out who all was in the kitchens that night. Sadly, there were several other people who could potentially be his match and the reality burst my bubble somewhat. Why couldn't I have been the only female in the room that night? Then there would be no question to my being his match.

Still, If it was meant to end, if I wasn't the one for

him, at least I'd get one more interaction to hold onto when I left. My stomach did a little flip at the idea, and for once, no one hassled me on my way home from the shuttle.

I walked up the rickety stairwell to our unit, listening to the sounds of poverty around me. Next door, the baby was crying over the din of television. Down the hall, the sound of shouted obscenities was punctuated by broken glass. Or maybe that was upstairs. It was impossible to tell which direction it came from when there was chaos and misery everywhere you looked.

No wonder I always wanted to escape reality and blur the lines of my life so that I lived in a somewhat fantasy world. It must have been a survival tactic of my mind, where it shut itself off when there was turmoil around me.

It was a far cry from the idyllic, rambling old farmhouse I'd grown up in, where Corinne and I had been born. Mom and Dad were both teachers, and while they placed a high value on learning, they raised us on the outskirts of the municipality, saying the best things for us were fresh air and space to roam, to explore.

There was a small creek that ran behind the house

and an apple tree that grew heavy every year with the fruit. I'd swim in the creek when the air was thick with heat and mosquitoes, and in the fall, when the apples were full and juicy, we'd gather them up and bake pies.

It had all been destroyed in a siege when I was eight, though, and now it was all a pile of ash. As ugly as anything here in the refugee precinct.

I yearned to have those times back. If I could only bite into a juicy, ripe, delicious apple one more time. If only I could run through the yard, giggling as the soft grass tickled my ankles and the gentle breeze billowed through my hair. It seemed like a million years ago, or even worse, that I had dreamed it all and had never experienced it in real life.

For years, I'd repressed all that pain. I didn't have time to deal with the loss, so I pushed it into a box and set it aside. Now, it almost felt like it had happened to someone else. I wasn't that innocent girl anymore and I never would be again. Times had changed. My demeanor had toughened. I'd survived against all odds, and it was my responsibility to ensure that Corinne did the same.

But, a tiny voice said, maybe I could still be happy. Perhaps there was some quiet and peaceful life out there, just waiting for me to find it.

I unlocked the door and went into our apartment, surprised the lights were all out. Everything was quiet and undisturbed. It was entirely unnatural. I reached out and waved my hand in front of the motion activation panel.

Nothing.

Had Corinne had another bad migraine? She had lessons today, but maybe she'd come home early and deactivated the lights. I knew bright lights tended to make her headaches worse. I searched my mind, trying to remember if she'd ever meddled with the lights before.

"Corinne?" I whispered.

Silence greeted me and gave me an ominously eerie feeling that prickled against my skin.

I stepped toward the wall to manually raise the lights and felt the sickly, unnatural crunch of glass underfoot. The sound sliced through my heart and I briefly froze like a deer in headlights.

My blood cooled in my veins and I felt the familiar rush of adrenaline course through me. On my own for so long, I had developed something of a sensitivity to danger. Threats often lurked in the dark, ready to pounce on the vulnerable.

I rushed to the wall then and pressed against the manual electrical control, but the light barely sparked to life. The overhead light source flickered, half dislodged from the ceiling, revealing a scene that sent chills of fear racing through me. I held my breath and waited. If there were an attacker here, they would be ready to pounce. More importantly, where was Corinne?

The place was trashed. But more alarming, from what I could see, the few possessions that might be considered of value to someone desperate enough were still in place. Why would someone rip through here like a tornado but take nothing?

The only thing missing, I realized as my eyes nervously surveyed the disorder, was Corinne. My throat stifled a scream. Panic ensued, shattering me to the bone.

Had someone followed her? The creep who had harassed me the day before, maybe? Bile rose in my throat at the thought, strangling the scream that wanted to escape. My breath came in uneven, raspy batches.

I was half tempted to march onto the street and track the bastard down, but some small fraction of reason was still in control. The reality was that I had absolutely no idea what had happened. I didn't owe any money to the local 'protection' posse, and as far as I knew, Corinne kept to her studies and didn't have any enemies. Who had broken in? Perhaps it was the wrong apartment, meant for someone else?

I reached for my phone quickly and started to call the authorities. Dread filled me. Emergency services were known to brush off reports of violence or criminal activity in our precinct as par for the course. If they responded to every single complaint, they'd never have time to do anything else. Still, it was my only hope. I had to report it, and my sister as missing.

Suddenly, a phone began to buzz on the counter, a phone I didn't recognize. A number I didn't know displayed, and I answered without hesitation, holding the phone to my ear and waiting. My ears prickled with dread as I waited expectantly for a voice to come through.

"You like my redecorating?" My heart stilled. It was Darla's voice. "I thought it was an improvement, but then, can you really dress trash up as anything else?" Her sinister laugh snickered coolly through the phone. Anger boiled my veins and nearly incinerated them.

"Where is she?" I demanded, even though my voice came out more broken than I wanted it to.

I didn't want to reveal that I was rattled, not in the slightest. If Darla knew I viewed her as a threat, she would have the upper hand. I didn't care what she did to my apartment. She could burn the damn thing down, for all I cared. I just wanted the assurance that my sister was safe.

She laughed, the cold sound sending spirals of terror through me. "Suddenly not so lippy, are you?"

I didn't answer, just waited, heart in my throat. I didn't want to move or breathe until she returned my sister.

"Corinne is fine. I have her somewhere safe. For now." Her tone was abstract, unrevealing.

"What do you want? Just tell me what I need to do —" I started. I hated the fact that I was begging, but I had no choice.

Darla cut in. "I want you gone."

"What do you mean?" I asked, confused. I shook my head as hot tears stung my eyes and blurred my vision.

"You'll get your sister back as long as you do everything I tell you to. First off, you're quitting. Bon voyage and all that shit. You'll hand in your resignation tomorrow. You'll tell everyone that another opportunity came up that was better for your family. Any questions, you answer them with something vague." Her tone was threatening as if there was no room or option for me to debate or protest her demands in any way.

"I . . ." I swallowed the lump in my throat, forcing myself to think only about Corinne. Nothing else mattered. Sacrifices would have to be made in order for her safe return. "Okay. I'll do it. Is that all?"

"No. You're not to reach out to the prince, at all, ever again. Do that, and you'll get Corinne back, unharmed." Her tone was so icy that it made me shiver.

There it was. the condition that knocked the wind out of me. I retched, but there was no food in my stomach to spew. I doubled over in pain.

It took a moment, but I finally answered. "I'll do anything. Just, please, don't hurt Corinne."

"Well, we'll see how well you keep your word, won't we?" she hissed with a devilish laugh that made my bones tingle. She was cold and calculated, but I had no choice but to adhere to her instructions if I ever wanted to see my sister alive again.

The line went dead then, and I collapsed, horrified at the nightmare that had just swallowed me up.

Choking sobs ravaged me and shook through my entire body. My shoulders went limp. My eyes were puffy and swollen. Eventually, I fell asleep, but the nightmare never left me. Even with sleep, I couldn't escape the harsh reality that was swirling around me.

CHAPTER 9

GARDAX

"Your breakfast, Your Highness."

I looked up from my reading to see a familiar face, but it wasn't Amy's. My heart had fluttered expectantly, but it wasn't her dreamy voice cooing seductively through my ears. It wasn't her cream-colored face and piercing eyes that stared through me. Disenchantment flared my nostrils.

I swallowed my disappointment and asked, "Has Miss Allen's reassignment gone smoothly?"

"Miss Allen?" the maid asked. "Oh! Amy? My apologies, Your Highness. No, Your Grace, she quit this morning."

The words struck me with unexpected force. I had to quickly recover so this person in front of me wouldn't see my emotions.

"She quit?" I repeated, the question feeling bitter in my mouth. I swallowed hard and tried not to engulf myself in the sea of yearning that I felt for Amy. I didn't even realize how much I was consumed by her until I realized she was gone.

"Yes, Your Highness, just a short time ago." The maid seemed confused by my line of questioning.

I started to rise. "So, she's still here?" I wasn't about to let her get away without an explanation. I needed more information. I needed to know a reason why. I had to find the source of why my heart ached and throbbed as if something had been ripped away from me, something I craved.

"Don't think so. She seemed to be in something of a hurry. Besides, I'm sure Darla made quick work of the matter," she said in a way that harkened to Amy's earlier comment about her supervisor's terrible personality.

A light bulb went off in my mind. "How do you know this?" I asked, stepping forward. I narrowed my eyes suspiciously.

The maid looked suddenly uncomfortable. She shifted her weight as if she were paranoid that she might reveal too much. "Well, we rode the shuttle in together this morning."

"Did she say why?" I pressed. I wasn't trying to rattle this particular maid, but I was desperate for answers.

She looked contemplative, scrunching her face. She was older, with a kind, gentle face. She had that maternal warmth about her, like she would be the type to wear an apron and tell funny stories while she stirred a warm pot of soup on the stove.

"Ehm. well, now that you ask, she didn't give a clear answer. Something about a job opportunity she couldn't turn down, good thing for her family or some such. She's got a little sister, you know. She's a good girl, Amy," she said, chatting more casually now that she realized I wasn't interrogating her.

"Yes, I know. Did she say where she was going to work?" I leaned closer and held my breath, hoping this woman would at least be able to point me in the right direction with her information.

"No. I can't say she mentioned it. Can't say it'd be hard to find a better position though," she started to say, as if partially to herself, before remembering where she was. "Oh! I didn't mean any offense, Your Highness. I just mean her supervisor. Well, she's a real battle-axe." She frowned as if she were afraid to divulge any other clues.

She proceeded to lift the lids off the many plates of food, the smell rising to tempt me but doing nothing to distract from the overwhelming disappointment that rocked me. I couldn't see straight. My vision clouded and all I wanted was to know where Amy went and the reason for her hasty disappearance.

"Is there anything else I can get for you, Your Highness?" she asked politely, oblivious to my distress. Her smile was warm and genuine.

"No." I shook my head. "That'll be all, thank you." I gave her a wan smile, but I was so distracted I hardly noticed her standing there anymore. My head was numb.

As soon as she left, I started making calls. First, to Amy's phone. *Pick up.* I mentally tried to send her telepathic waves. *Please. Pick up the phone.*

But every call went unanswered, and I racked my brain, wondering what had happened and finding no reasonable explanation. Granted, I didn't know Amy that well yet, but something told me she wasn't the type to intentionally avoid my calls unless something was terribly amiss.

I needed answers. Something wasn't sitting well with my psyche about this situation. It was like that natural instinct that kicked in to alert your mind that something wasn't adding up.

Unfortunately, Coel didn't have them for me. He was as surprised by her resignation as I was.

"I am notified of any changes in staffing and I haven't received any information from her superior," he started with a quizzical and perplexed tone.

"Darla! Yes, that's right, her supervisor. Check in with her and see if she has a way to contact Amy. I want to know what's going on," I directed him, not caring if I sounded desperate.

Coel nodded and headed out, already determined and on a mission.

Frustrated, restless, I paced the great hall. It was foolish, but if she was still there, it seemed like the best place to run into her. I ran a shaky hand through my dark hair. I wasn't used to being so affected by a woman of any kind. I needed to make sure that Amy was safe, at the very least. I wouldn't rest until I had that reassuring information.

I looked down through the transparent floor beneath my feet at the city below, wondering where she was down there, wondering what was going on in her mind. I didn't know her well, that was true, but I knew enough to know that I hadn't imagined the attraction between us. Maybe I had responded to her more than she had to me, that was possible, but I knew it wasn't entirely one-sided. The heat and chemistry radiated between us. The vibrations were hard to deny.

"Your Highness!" A voice came from behind me and I spun around. The voice sounded squeaky and frantic.

It was the woman who had confronted me in the kitchens, Darla. "Mrs. Barnaby," I said, acknowledging her with a swift nod.

She came closer, uncomfortably close. "I understand you're trying to track down Amy Allen?" Her eyebrows were raised, and her expression was that of a shark hunting its prey. I took a step backward.

"Yes. Yes, I am. Do you have some way to reach her?" I asked eagerly. It might have occurred to others to mask their emotion, but I'd never mastered the art nor had any interest in doing so. I was an open book. I told it like it was, regardless of how it made others feel inside.

Her face broke into a smile that seemed completely out of place on her and insincere. Her expression was wild, almost wicked.

"I do, Your Highness. She left me a number for her new place, she said, in case anyone wanted to reach out to her. She thought that might be the case," she said, handing me a slip of paper before continuing on, "Put me in quite a lurch, you know, but she was bound and determined that she couldn't work here another day." She scoffed in a feigned resentful way and waved her bony hand through the air.

The writing was sloppy and difficult to read, but I pulled my phone out and dialed the number, not really listening to Darla's continued chatter. I didn't care what she had to say. I just wanted to hear Amy's voice, to know that she was okay.

"This line has been disconnected. Please try again or contact Union Star Communications at 1-700—" I hung up and tried again, shaking my head with increasing frustration.

Over and over, the same message. It was mocking me and taunting me. My throat was closing in, making it difficult to swallow and draw in a breath.

I didn't understand. Had I offended her? I looked through the messages we had exchanged the day before. Had I said something wrong? Did I misread her responses? I had thought she understood my playful tone. was I mistaken? Had I offended her? I had a million questions racing through my brain and no answers to pacify my shrieking mind.

I slumped back against the wall, replaying our conversation. My mind was trying to pick at the tiny fibers in the tangled web of confusion. What had I done to make Amy retreat like this?

"No answer?" Darla asked, coming close again and putting an ice-cold hand to my arm. The contact felt wrong and I tried to politely pull away without giving any emotion away that her cold touch repulsed me and felt violating.

"No. it seems the number isn't in operation," I answered, then looked to her, wondering what she knew. "Did she say anything to you about being unhappy here?" My voice was robotic.

She brushed a stray lock of pale blonde hair out of her face, tucking it behind her ear as she looked up at me with a certain sparkle that sent warning flags flying in my mind. Something sinister was twirling in her brain.

"She didn't say much, but she must be out of her mind. You know, I hope I don't sound too forward, but just between us, I don't know what she could possibly have been unhappy about. This place, this job. You. Well, I'm sure you don't need to be told, but you're a dream come true." She giggled but it came out sounding more like a cackle from a deranged animal.

My throat felt dry. I didn't want to accept these compliments from her. *She* was definitely not the person I wanted to hear say these things. Besides, wasn't she married? Why was she acting so flirtatious with me? Why didn't she care more about Amy's whereabouts? More importantly, would she not have to know exactly where she had gone?

"Right, well if you hear from her, please let my security team know. It's very important that I speak to her. I appreciate your assistance, *Mrs.* Barnaby." I left an emphasis on the subtle fact that she was married.

Her shrewd eyes flickered with irritation. "I doubt I'll hear anything from her. She got what she could out of this position." Her expression softened, and in a voice probably meant to sound wise but that came across as cruel and biting, she added, "I'm sure you're not used to dealing with such low classes of people, but Amy is a certain sort of person. She came from the gutter, and no matter what she does, she'll end up right back there. It's just where she belongs."

Her tone, her words, the look of disgust on her face as she said it all sparked an unexpected anger in me. How dare this woman speak so vile about a hard-working, brave person like Amy? She knew nothing of Amy's personal struggle. My emotions were tattered and raw.

I squared my jaw and coolly responded, "It would seem we have differing opinions on the matter, Mrs. Barnaby." I narrowed my eyes on hers, expecting a reaction.

Before she could answer and before I lost my temper, I strode past her and down the hall. I couldn't look back. I had work to do, and clearly, Darla was going to be a bump in the road, blocking my path.

"Your Highness," Coel alerted me. "The women have been assembled."

"Right." I nodded. "I'll be there in a moment." I took a deep breath and fretfully paced the room.

My motivation was sapped and my enthusiasm all but nonexistent. I wasn't interested in entertaining anyone. I was drained and frustrated.

It had been two days and I had no idea where she had

gone. Somehow, we didn't have her residence information and none of her coworkers seemed to have
interacted with her outside of their work here. She
couldn't have just vanished into thin air. Somebody
knew where she was. Someone out there had the
information I needed, and they were hiding it from
me deliberately.

There were moments where I almost wondered if I
had hallucinated the whole thing. But I had her file, I
had her story, and I had the brief interaction we had
shared. It wasn't much to go on, though, and I knew I
should respect her decision to leave, even if it jarred
me in unexpected ways.

I just hadn't been expecting her to disappear. I
thought we had shared something special, even if I
couldn't pinpoint what it was other than the fact that
I felt euphoria whenever we were engaged in conversation. Something in the back of my mind led me to
believe that she might be in trouble, but without a
solid lead, I was powerless to help her.

Coel had gathered the women from the kitchen—the
ones still here, anyway—and I would meet each,
conduct a brief interview, and discreetly check to see
if they set off the scanner. Secretly, I hoped that none
of them were a match.

I had read through all of their backgrounds. None of

them ignited me. None of them fascinated or captivated me the way Amy had. But, apparently, she
hadn't felt it the way I did. I had imagined our chemistry. I had read into her subtle hints of flirtation in
the wrong way.

And I had a duty to honor. It was important for me
to find the *genetic* match, not the one who made me
feel like I was floating on a cloud of bliss. If I wanted
to save my species, I had to let go of the desires of
my heart.

I walked with Coel to the leisure deck. During long
space voyages, it was where I spent the bulk of my
time. It held my library which contained tomes from
a vast array of alien civilizations, as well as the
greatest works of Trilyn culture and history. I loved to
wade through this wealth of information, learning as
much as I could about the culture which I prided and
held dear to my heart.

It also held a number of state rooms for diplomatic
entertainment. It was here I waited as Coel left to
usher in the first candidate. I stood proudly and
stiffly, anticipating how these interviews would go. If
I didn't exhibit any kind of enthusiasm, it was bound
to fail even if I found my match.

In walked the first girl. With closely cropped green
hair, almond eyes, and delicate features, she was quite

pretty in an edgy, ethereal way. In fact, she looked like someone I might have met in Erebis.

But she wasn't Amy and I felt nothing but civility toward her. We chatted politely about inconsequential matters, the ship, Trilyn tech, and so on. After a suitable time had passed, I thanked her for her time. The conversation hadn't flowed naturally like it had with Amy. There was no witty banter. It was professional and robotic.

She smiled sadly. "Not my lucky day, then, eh?"

Despite neither of us broaching the subject, it was there nonetheless, and I appreciated her candor. My scanner had a negative reading and I responded earnestly in kind. "No, I'm sorry to disappoint you."

"Well, I hope you find her," she answered in a hushed whisper. Her eyes flashed with sorrow and for a flickering of a second, I felt sympathy for her.

"You and me both." I smiled warmly. The girl was nice, but she wasn't the one.

An hour later, Coel had ushered in two more employees and each of them induced no positive results from the scanner. For some reason, these realizations gave me a sense of false hope and relief.

It didn't surprise me, but it did frustrate me that I

wouldn't have the opportunity to interview the one person I really wanted to see. I knew my own feelings meant nothing in the face of what I needed to do for my people, but my focus wasn't on that. My thoughts were somewhere in the city below, with a certain redhead I couldn't manage to forget. Until I knew why and where she had gone, I knew I wouldn't rest easily. She was out there somewhere. I had the technology and resources to find her. I just needed to brainstorm the perfect plan for initiating that dream.

CHAPTER 10

AMY

"**A**re you okay? Is she feeding you?" I asked, jittery as I spoke to Corinne over the cheap phone Darla had left for me. My voice was nervous and trembling. I didn't want Corinne to be able to feel my fear. I needed to be strong and resilient to keep us both going.

One of her conditions was that I get rid of my previous phone, cutting off all chances for Gardax to reach me. I didn't understand what had possessed her to do this, but it didn't matter. All that mattered was that I get Corinne away from her in one piece. Nothing else mattered until I had Corinne safely back under the umbrella and protection of my embrace.

"Yeah, I'm eating," Corinne answered, her voice

barely above a whisper. She sounded weak and far away.

I strained my ears for background noise, but I couldn't pick up anything. It was the same series of questions every night. Darla gave me a few minutes to check with Corinne every night, to flaunt her leverage, I'm sure, but it was enough to keep me going. As long as I knew that Corinne was still alive, that was all the fuel I needed to press forward.

"All right, you dumpster scrap, that's enough. Your sister is alive and intact. Hold up your end," Darla barked into the phone.

Anger coiled in my throat and I wanted to rage, I wanted to scream, to let loose every ounce of hate and wrath that I was suppressing, but I didn't. I couldn't. I hadn't protected Corinne all these years to fail now. If I made one false move, I'd sabotage her safety.

"Please. Just please, don't hurt her. She's all I have," I begged instead. I was pitiful and desperate under the clutches of Darla's powerful grip. The worst part was that she was relishing in having this authority over me and my actions.

"Let's keep it that way," she said cryptically before

hanging up with a harsh click that left my ears ringing. The jolt back to silence was deafening.

I collapsed onto the sofa bed, feeling more alone than ever before. I was tired in my mind and my bones. I just wanted to fall asleep and wake up again, praying that this had all been a nightmare and that Corinne would be staring at me when I opened my eyes.

My stomach grumbled. I hadn't eaten all day. I'd been too busy out searching for another job and coming up empty. Without a recommendation from my last employer, the jobs that were already scarce were practically impossible to get.

Worried as I was about getting Corinne back, I was worried too about what would happen to us. Without any income flowing in, I was going to quickly eat through the meager savings I had amassed. The prospects of finding something before I completely ran out of resources was looking bleaker by the second.

I walked over to the ancient refrigerator that came with our unit. The light had gone out and I didn't have the money to spend to replace it. Not that it mattered. I didn't need a light to tell me it was almost empty. I fumbled with my hand and squinted through the darkness, searching for anything that I could scrape a meal together with.

I grabbed the last package of tofu and pulled it out, ripping the cover off and eating it cold. I didn't have the energy to dress it up. Besides, it was going to taste bland and like cardboard no matter how I tried to make it fancy.

It was flavorless and spongey, but it was sustenance, and I wasn't in a position to turn up my nose at that. I only hoped Corinne was eating enough as well. She'd always been on the skinny side and small for her age. I tried not to think about it too much, but deep down, I blamed myself. If Darla wasn't feeding her, it would enrage me.

I was a good four inches taller than her at that age, and I couldn't help but to think it was because she'd grown up surviving on scraps, whereas I had lived the first formative years fairly well, provided for by our parents.

And now, she was in the clutches of that horrid wretch and that was probably my fault as well. I muddled through the theories in my mind. What could I have done differently? What kind of situations had I inadvertently placed myself in to lead to these mistakes? Now Corinne was the one paying the price.

I sighed, exhausted, still hungry, and depressed. I

tried to force back the hot tears stinging my eyes. I swallowed hard and took a deep, shaky breath.

Lying down again, I listened to the sounds of the city outside and looked out the window. It was dark, and I could just make out the stars through the smog from the city overhead. Somewhere up there, hidden in the night sky, invisible to my naked eyes, was Gardax . Was he thinking about me? Was he wondering what kind of fate had befallen me? Was he ready to search for me?

I wondered if he thought anything of my leaving. I'd managed to avoid him when I dropped off my notice. Darla had insisted I come in, make a presence, and put to rest any questions about my leaving. But I had been terrified that I'd run into him and that I wouldn't be able to lie, and Corinne would pay the price.

For some reason, I had the sneaking suspicion that I couldn't lie to him. I wanted so desperately to contact him, to at least explain that I didn't have a choice. Of course, that was probably making much more out of it than there was. He had seemed interested, but he was a prince, after all. I doubted he would have any trouble moving on. By now, he'd probably completely forgotten about me. He was probably back to using his scanner to find his real soulmate.

I closed my eyes, retreating to that secret space that felt further away now than ever before, and slowly drifted away. Sleep came easily to me now, thankfully, because I was too exhausted for my mind to protest.

I was dressed in silks. Delicate, sleek robes embroidered with glittering designs that sparkled as brightly as starlight. In fact, everything around me was lit by a warm, soft haze. I had a shimmering feeling as if I were tingling like a butterfly floating in the wind. A warm sensation encompassed me, and I was filled with euphoria.

Looking around, I was in a chamber I didn't recognize but somehow felt vaguely familiar. In front of me was a massive bed, enclosed by sheer curtains that glowed with a luminescence all their own. It was the biggest bed I'd ever seen, and I ached to fall into its massive cushions. It appeared so plush, welcoming, and inviting that it lured me in a tranquil way.

Someone cleared their throat behind me, and in an instant, I knew where I was. I turned around, smiling at the familiar sight of him. He studied my body with those striking, otherworldly yellow eyes of his and came toward me. His movements were seductive and made my heart race.

"Of all the worlds I've crossed, you're the most beautiful thing I've ever seen," he purred into my ear as he snaked two arms around my waist. I melted into his warm embrace, surrendering to the freedom and safety he brought to me just with his simple touch.

I sighed against the firm strength of his hands, his arms, his chest that crushed against mine. Being next to him felt natural. I felt his heart pounding in his chest, rhythmically pulsing in unison with mine.

"Where are we?" I asked, a little breathless, my senses fuzzy. I didn't care. As long as I was with him, I was in a heavenly state of mind.

He quirked a smile. "This is our bed, my love. It was mine, and now it is *ours*. Come, let us introduce the two of you. You should get acquainted, as I have no intention of letting you out of it anytime soon." His voice was a prayer song that sang alluringly to my heart.

Bending down, Gardax snaked a hand beneath me and lifted me up, pushing aside the sheer curtains and carrying me to the middle of the massive bed. A smile cracked across my lips. His gentle touch pacified me.

My body screamed when he laid me down and pulled back. Instinctively, I reached out, but he caught my hands.

"Ah, ah, ah. Patience. We have a lifetime to give into our passions. But this, I want to savor this," he said, raising a hand to my cheek and staring so deeply into my eyes, I thought I might just melt into the cushion right there. I took deep breaths, a wild hunger brewing inside me.

He dipped gently toward me, and our lips met, heat radiating throughout my whole body and settling in spots too long forgotten. I yearned for him, craved his touch against my skin. I wanted him to ravage me and explore my body in all the secret and forbidden spots.

His mouth on mine, I braced myself, holding onto the strong frame of his wide, muscular shoulders. My grip was poor, though, as my hands were no match for the rounded bulk of his muscles. I fumbled to keep my grip on him. I never wanted to let him go.

Gardax's mouth made its way to my neck, and I raised my hands to his neck, hooking them there and clinging to him against the wave of awareness that was overtaking me. His breath was cool on my neck, sending prickles of pleasure up my spine.

My breathing hitched, and I felt a wet heat pool between my legs as his mouth found my breasts. The fabric between us seemed to dissipate and I felt scorched by him everywhere. His mouth was perfec-tion as he grazed his gentle lips against my skin, sending me into a hysteria of passionate longing.

"I want to taste you now," he murmured against my stomach. His voice was hungry and desperate.

"Yes," I barely managed through the suspense. I arched my back and pressed myself against him.

My hands coiled in the thick jet-black locks of his hair that were just long enough to grab onto. I was so wobbly with pleasure that I was certain if I let go of him, I'd slip through the cracks and land in a less blissful place. He dipped forward, parting my folds with his tongue, and my whole body shuddered in response. A croak bubbled in my throat and escaped my lips as a sigh.

"Mmm, delicious," he whispered as he laved. His tongue was making perfect circles on my pulsing, engorged places.

Hooking both his arms around my thighs, he lifted me up to him, putting me in the incredibly erotic position of being open and vulnerable to him. I was spread wide, gleaming with a wetness derived from his seductive touch.

I gasped and gripped at the bed beneath me, but nothing brought relief as he relentlessly circled the tight bud of my sensation. Every nerve in my body seemed to ignite, and I looked up at him, desperate and hungry for release. Our eyes locked, and that was it. I was drowning, lost. Perspiration prickled on my skin. Intense heat flushed my cheeks. My thighs began to shake in reaction to the exotic pleasure he brought between my legs.

Everything went out of focus and it felt like I was drifting away until my body brought me back, the awareness of being parted by something different, something new. My pulse flashed between my legs, and a puddle of passion flooded me, soaking the sheets beneath me.

It was my first time, and I opened my eyes once more to find him watching me, studying me with adoration and curiosity as if he loved the way I blossomed and he loved the taste of my fruits.

Only he wasn't there. I was staring up at the dingy ceiling of my apartment once more, tears wetting my cheeks. It had only been a dream. But it had felt so real. I was still shaking in the euphoria of his tongue swirling between my legs.

It was too real, too transporting to have been just a dream. My body ached, but more importantly, so did my heart. I felt between my legs. I was swollen down there, the bridge between dream land and reality. My fingers came back ripe and juicy, a little damp. I had nothing to show for the reaction. I was alone in a silent apartment that was burdened with poverty.

Dawn splashed light across the room and I looked around at the shambles surrounding me. It was a crushing blow to be back in a nightmare of reality. I didn't even have Corinne by my side to talk to and comfort ourselves with each other's company.

I don't know if it was the dream, if it was the desperation of my situation, or if it was just the emotions I had held at bay for too long, always shutting down in the interest of self-preservation, but something possessed me. There was a burning flame igniting my soul.

I reached out and grabbed my phone, punching in Gardax's number, the digits I had committed to memory before I got rid of my previous phone. I was proud of myself for taking the initiative to know his number by heart. The dream had been so vivid, so consuming. I yearned to hear his voice, and in the heat of my saturated desire, I was fueled by enough bravery to make the plunge and call him.

It chimed, telling me it was ringing, and the harsh, shrill sound was enough to bring me back to my senses. I pulled it away and hung up in an instant, staring at it like some kind of evil relic capable of destroying me. My breath froze in my throat. I was unable to move for a second, rooted to the floor.

And then it rang.

My heart leaped in my throat and then died. It was Darla. How was this happening? Electricity sent volts of panic through my mind, sending me on a tailspin through darkness.

"Tsk, tsk, Amy, that wasn't a good idea. I thought I was clear. Do I need to be more explicit?" she asked. Her voice was high, demanding, and shrill.

How did she even know? I searched my mind for the possibilities.

I closed my eyes, angry, hurt, overwhelmed. "No. I'm sorry, it was a mistake. I won't do it again, I promise." I didn't have any excuses to give her. It wouldn't do me any good anyway. I'd been singled out, caught in the act.

"You're lucky I'm in a good mood this morning. And you're lucky he didn't answer. If he had, I'd have been forced to cut off two of Corinne's bony little fingers and I just don't feel like cleaning up that kind of mess today, so don't push me, Amy. Don't fucking push me. This is your last warning."

Her hostile voice sliced through my heart. My knees buckled, and I crashed to the floor in a heap of despair. How could she be so sadistic and twisted? Was she just bluffing? I didn't want to test the waters and find out.

I sat for a long while after, just staring at nothing, seeing only the scarlet red of my own anger and wishing I knew how to use it against her. I would have to brainstorm a way to get back at her. I didn't even know where to start. I had no idea where she was storing Corinne.

I imagined her in some dark cell or dank, musty dungeon somewhere. The fury boiled in my blood and burned my skin. I cracked my knuckles. Darla must have had some kind of tracking sensor device placed in my phone to monitor ingoing and outgoing calls. I fumbled with the phone, trying my best to tear it apart, but it was no use. Darla was winning the battle, but I had to find a way to destroy her.

CHAPTER 11

GARDAX

"**Y**our Highness, may I present La'Trisha Theodopolous," Coel announced with an enthusiastic bellowing voice.

I yawned before the young lady stepped out from behind Coel's wide frame. It was early, but I had to get this business over with and move on. Unrest on Erebis was fomenting and I was eager to return soon, but I couldn't exactly do so empty-handed. I wasn't interested in any of these women, but I had to appease them nonetheless.

La'Trisha moved into the room. She was much prettier than her photograph had represented, with a halo of tightly curled coils of black hair and warm, open eyes. Like the others from the afternoon before, she seemed a bundle of nervous excitement. She shifted her weight and stared at me with huge round eyes and an expectant expression.

I smiled politely and waved her toward a seat opposite me. "Please join me, Ms. Theodopolous." My demeanor was formal and my tone was professional.

"Thank you, Your Majesty!" she chirped, her voice colored by a faint rasp. Her cheeks blushed at the direct attention I gave to her.

I sighed. "I assume you know why you're here." I interlocked my fingers and stared at her.

"Because we might be biologically compatible, yes." She nodded as if she understood completely but had that dreamy, internal hope that she might be the match.

"What do you think of it?" I asked. More and more, these meetings were beginning to feel a bit dirty and one-sided. Amy's disappearance had provoked my reflection on the matter. Beyond wealth, what was I offering? It just made the entire ordeal superficial. These women didn't want me for my personality. They wanted my wealth and status.

I needed to know how these women felt about it. It occurred to me that I had made wild assumptions about the fact that, once found, my perfect match would just willingly abandon everything to start a life with me on another planet. I had been forced to reconcile myself to the idea that this process was going to be rather un-romantic, but I'd had time to adjust to the matter. It was a lot to ask of a woman to give up her entire life and family, all for a stranger residing on a different planet across the galaxy.

She looked at me with confusion. "Think of what, Your Majesty?" Her pouty lips pursed with perplexity.

"Well, if I turn this scanner on and it says you're the match for me, do you have any opinion on the subject? Would it frighten you?" I asked, not really sure where I was going with these questions but too tired and frustrated to stop. They had to know what they were getting into, anyway. I might as well raise the subject.

"Well," she said, crossing her legs in front of her, "I suppose I'd feel lucky? It's not every day a girl gets engaged to a prince. But, no, I don't think it would scare me or else I wouldn't have come, right?" she asked rhetorically. I couldn't tell if she was lying or just making something up that she thought I might find appealing and approving.

"So you'll have no qualms with the arrangement?" I prodded further with a raised, cynical eyebrow.

"Can I speak honestly?" she asked. Her voice lowered, and she leaned in closer to me.

"Please do," I urged. Honesty was always the best policy, especially in a situation such as this.

"Well, I guess I would hope we could get to know each other a little better first. No offense, but you're not sending me any particularly hot vibes right now. While the idea of living in some crazy alien palace sounds awesome, I'd hope there could be some sort of spark to build from," she said, looking unsure. She was right, of course. Pretty and polite as she may be, I had no gut reaction to our meeting. If anything, I respected her more after her admittance, and she stuck out from the rest by being so forthright in her honesty.

I nodded. "And if there were none? If I asked you to leave your home and everything you've ever known behind and become my bride, my queen, to bear my children and embrace my people, could you do all that, with or without the presence of mutual affection?" I didn't see how anyone could ever say yes to the questions I posed, especially when they were phrased as bluntly as I had hashed them out.

La'Trisha looked thoughtful for a moment, surveying the finely furnished room around her with its transparent wall that overlooked the dark depths of space beyond the blue haze of planetary atmosphere. It was as common as seeing a sunset now.

"Damn, you put a girl on the spot." She finally laughed, causing me to smile. "I don't know. I guess I'd have to think about it then." She shrugged apologetically and blushed again, having difficulty making eye contact with me. She sniffed, and there was an awkward silence.

"Thank you for your honesty," I replied. "Well, then, shall we give it a go?" I asked in a peppier voice. I didn't want to dampen the party of my current company any further.

"Let's do it," she agreed and then, jittery, laughed. "Whew, pressure's on!" She took a deep breath and leaned back, rubbing the perspiration off her brow.

I pressed my finger into the gooey identification pad and the device came to life. I set it on the low table between us and waited, both of us staring at it nervously. My heart pounded in my chest, but the air in my lungs felt paralyzed. I didn't move or flinch. Out of the corner of my eye, I noticed that La'Trisha was also as still and frozen as a statue.

Nothing happened, and my pulse picked up suddenly. If it wasn't her, then that left only two remaining candidates. I waited a second more, but the device did nothing. There were no bells, flashes, or whistles, only silence.

After a moment, La'Trisha looked up. "I take it we didn't hit the jackpot." Her voice sounded mildly disappointed.

"No, I'm sorry." I shook my head. "But I appreciate your coming down here and speaking openly with me." I gave her a regretful smile of chagrin and shook her hand.

She smiled nonchalantly. "To tell you the truth, I'm a little relieved." I guess I hadn't sold the situation or myself very well in the beginning, but it was just as well. I still had only one woman on my mind, and at the moment, she was missing.

I laughed then. "Please explain, and don't spare my feelings." I paused and waited for La'Trisha to elaborate.

La'Trisha stood, smoothing out the skirt of her uniform. "Everything you described sounds like a lot of pressure. To tell the truth, I hadn't really thought it through quite that far. I mean, hey, you seem nice, and you've got a pretty nice place here, but I'm gonna need a little more to go on. Something tells me," she said, studying me, "well, it just seems like your heart's not in it."

"Astute," I agreed and thanked her as Coel led her out. She'd hit the nail on the head, and I appreciated her honesty about the situation. She wasn't fake or phony, but she also wasn't my biological and genetic match. On to the next one.

After she left, I pulled up the files of my last two candidates. Of course, it had come down to them. On one hand, there was the girl of my dreams, literally. On the other, a woman whose presence I could barely stomach. I didn't even notice that my hands were shaking. A lot was on the line here, and I had so much riding on what would come of the device and its response to the next candidates.

The thought of bringing Darla up here after her cloying behavior, her derision, and her insults toward Amy, made me nauseous. I couldn't even anticipate what I might do if she ended up being my match. Could I deny her anyway?

I knew it was technically possible she could be my match, but every time I imagined any sort of physical intimacy, it left a foul taste in my mouth and a sense of guilt, like I'd be betraying my own conscience in the process. I had heard now from several employees that she was not the best of supervisors. What would she be like with real power, as my queen? She gave me an unsettled feeling, and that was never a good start.

Status and position could corrupt even the most modest and humble of souls, and Darla was a far cry from that. Could I sacrifice my integrity for the sake of my people? Would it be worth it in the end? I shook my head and squeezed my eyes shut.

I was worrying over something that had not even happened yet. I didn't need to focus on any kind of anxiety of the future reaction of the scanner until I stared at the reality of it in the face. Until then, I would just have to ease my churning stomach with the concept that it probably wasn't going to be Darla as my perfect biological match.

Coel came in. "Would you like me to summon Mrs. Barnaby?" Even his voice was reluctant.

That's right, she was married. Given the way she'd flirted with and behaved around me, I suspected she wouldn't consider it a particular hurdle. Further argument against her. How would we even assume to take on a role as partners if she already had a spouse? It was enough to make me queasy and concocted a dull migraine in my head.

I shook my head. "No. Not today." I couldn't face it. I didn't have the stomach for it. It was either that, or unconsciously, I didn't want to know.

He looked surprised. "But she's the last candidate." He eyed me curiously.

"Not the last," I answered. "Gather a team, Coel. I need you to track down Amy Allen. I don't think I can face the possibility of Darla being my bride until I know, conclusively, that Amy isn't the one. I . . . I just need to know, for certain." It was a demand, a direct order. Not even Darla herself could stop me.

"As you wish, Your Highness," Coel said, bowing and marching off, the metal click of his armored boots echoing after him. He would never protest against me. He was loyal and respected me as his prince.

THE HOURS TICKED BY WHILE I WAITED FOR something, some information about Amy's whereabouts. I tried to read, but every book I picked up seemed to be a love story. I tried to work on state business but every missive I reviewed reminded me that everyone in Erebis, Trilynia itself, was waiting for me to find my bride. I paced the halls, but every corner I rounded, I caught myself hoping to see her. I couldn't distract myself, no matter how desperately I tried to immerse myself in some kind of engaging activity.

It was too much. I needed to distract myself, but it seemed impossible since I'd tried to discover every outlet imaginable. Every time I closed my eyes, all I could see was Amy's red hair and her genuine smile. Her gentle laugh tickled my soul. I desperately craved to find her. She had to be the one, but somehow, it just felt too good to be true that the person I had a spiritual connection with would also be my genetic match.

I went to my training room, forced my attention onto something else, something I could control, something that had nothing to do with Amy. I could allow my thoughts to center and escape in there.

The simulator spat attackers out at me, one after another. And one after another, I threw myself at them, pouring all of my energy into the fight. I sliced through the bodies of a dozen Durfa warriors, impaled a Yakat feeder, and went hand to hand with three rabid Cretorians. The energy and the fighting were therapeutic but not stimulating enough to keep my thoughts off Amy.

Their simulated blood and gore dissipated the instant my victory was won, and at the end of the session, I was alone in the vacuous, dark chamber, haunted once more by the thought that Amy might have been my match and I had let her slip away. How could I have made such a crucial mistake?

I climbed into the cleansing chamber, hoping the shock of water would drive the thoughts from my mind, but as I stood there, water flushing over my skin, I imagined her there with me. It wasn't hard to conjure a fantasy of what she would look like, what she might feel like. My body hardened in response and I pressed my head to the rounded glass wall, wondering if this was all I'd have of her. I didn't want to suffer a life with a bride that I had no deep connection with. I wanted Amy, plain and simple.

"I'VE GOT AN ADDRESS," COEL SAID, COMING INTO my private chamber early the next morning with no preamble.

I leapt to my feet. "Are you sure it's hers?" I asked anxiously. My pulse pounded through my ears.

He nodded. "I got a positive identification from a vagrant who says he's seen her coming and going from a complex for refugees in the precinct she was last registered in. With your permission, I'll escort her back to the ship to be presented to Your Highness." Coel sounded proud of himself for getting this far along the mission requested of him.

I shook my head, pulling on clothing. "No. Thank you. You've done excellent work, but this is one conversation I think I'd prefer to have myself."

Coel didn't argue. As the head of my security, it was not unusual for him to fight me on matters of safety, but as my assistant and friend for the past decade, he also knew well when I was beyond reasoning. It was no use. I would get what I wanted in the end.

As we climbed into a transport shuttle down to the city, my heart raced. I needed answers, but I was also worried they wouldn't be the ones I'd hoped for. I had to know. My heart drove me to find out.

If she was the one and she wanted nothing to do with me, if the life I proposed wasn't something she could sign on for, I understood. I would respect her wishes. But, one way or another, I was going to get an explanation. I thought at the very least, she owed me that. I could get the closure I needed to move on, but this wasn't over yet.

CHAPTER 12

AMY

My toes felt frozen and I woke up to the sensation of being stabbed by a thousand pins and needles in my arm. I had passed out in the same position that I had fallen into when I collapsed onto the sofa-bed. I must have been out cold for hours.

I tried to shake the sensation off, but it lingered, nerves firing up and down my arm and into my side. My hand trembled as I went to rehydrate my coffee granules. I took a deep breath, but it felt shaky. I was out of my element, feeling loopy and melancholy.

You can't keep this up much longer and you know it.

I was hardly sleeping, barely eating, and spending my time wrapped in a tight coil of worry. Not that self-care was something I'd ever been good about, but this was stretching the limits of what my body could take. But what choice did I have? It wasn't as if I had any fresh ideas on how to retrieve my sister, safe and sound and in one piece.

No one had need for an unreferenced refugee domestic worker, and with the stress of knowing money was going to dry up soon along with the constant fear for Corinne's wellbeing looming over me, it was hard to focus. I was nearing the breaking point. I felt like I was stumbling into brick wall after brick wall with no relief, or no break in the clouds on my destitute horizon.

Steam drifted in front of my face, carrying with it the distinctive smell of sweet caffeine, my only friend these days. I ripped into a pack of cheap salt-crackers and made the most out of the meager meal. I could hardly taste them on my tongue. The only thing I could taste lately was the brink of disaster and the gloomy bleakness of my future. I tried not to let my situation rob me of happiness, but what was there to feel joy about? I was immobilized and stagnant, wishing for a reunion with Corinne that I feared would never come.

It was the wrong time to think about it, but I couldn't help remembering all the delicious smells and foods in the kitchens on Gardax's ship. True, I'd rarely gotten to eat anything there. Darla would have flayed any of us alive for sneaking a bite, but occasionally, something would burn or come out wrong and the staff would get a taste of the good stuff.

My mouth watered at the memory and my stomach growled. I was creeping into starvation mode. All I had to do was feel my bones poking through my skin and the pang of hunger in my gut to realize that.

If only it was the food that I missed most, but it wasn't. Dreams of Gardax invaded even my waking hours—a symptom, perhaps, of the sleep deprivation. Maybe it was just my mind trying to gently nudge me back to a place where I wasn't teetering on the edge of self-destruction. If I could cloud my mind with fantasy, the vibrant spark inside me would remain alive.

What passed for my breakfast finished, I got changed and brushed the frizz and tangles out of my hair. I looked into the tiny mirror to redo my braid when my phone went off. I jumped a few inches. I wasn't expecting the shrill noise to come out of nowhere and pierce the crippling, maddening silence encompassing me.

Panic flushed through me and I jumped across the room to grab it, sending the brush clattering onto the cold, hard floor. Every time my phone rang, I clung to the desperate hope that it would be Darla, telling me that I could have my sister back. It was far-fetched, but I had to hold onto my resolve of hope.

"Hello?" I asked, fear and exhaustion making my voice tremble.

"Get out," Darla's voice demanded. "Get out of your apartment now!" The warning was harsh and slayed me.

I wasn't sure I heard her right. Her voice was barely above a whisper. Why was she being so quiet? What was going on? Fresh panic robbed my throat of receiving any breaths.

"What are you talking about?" I asked, sure I misunderstood her. I shook my head and frowned with anxiety.

"You have five minutes, maybe less. Get out of the apartment now, or I swear by all that is holy that I'll go and stick a knife right into Corinne's throat." Her tone was wicked and evil.

My stomach lurched and I tried to breathe. In shock, I looked around me, wondering what I had time to grab. It wasn't the first time I'd had to evacuate on a dime, and by now, I'd learned what was most crucial. I had no idea why Darla was sending me out of my house, but I knew enough about her harsh demands to know that I needed to abide by them, blindly, at all costs.

"Can I come back?" I asked, worrying over mine and Corinne's refugee documents. Without them, it was like the last ten years hadn't happened. We'd have to start all over from scratch. I didn't want to have to start all over. I wanted to know that I could come back here. It was the only roof over my head.

"No. Now *move!*" she hissed as if it wasn't up for debate and she was losing patience.

I ran to the sofa bed then, and holding the phone with my shoulder to my ear, I reached under and grabbed the avocado green metal lock box. Throwing open the lid, I grabbed the stash of documents, mine and Corinne's lives written out from start to finish on a few precious pieces of paper. If I couldn't come back, that meant I couldn't leave without them.

"Are you out yet?" Darla asked, panic coloring her voice. Her tone was like a deafening siren wailing through the night.

Whatever had her scared must be serious, and I wasn't about to stick around and find out what it was. If it was enough to spook a hardened woman like

Darla, that was enough to make me scatter like the gutter rats that roamed the hallways of this building.

I thrust my feet into my sturdiest boots and grabbed my coat. "Almost," I responded with a grunt as I pushed myself back into a standing position.

Glancing one last time behind me at the place that had been mine and Corinne's home for the last few years, I felt a bittersweet pang of remorse. How many homes would I have to abandon in an instant without warning like this? Would I ever have a home that lasted? I turned around and swallowed the sour feeling. Without Corinne, this wasn't home anymore anyway.

But there wasn't time to dwell. I slammed the door behind me and went to the stairwell. I sagged my shoulders with fleeting relief that it appeared to be empty, for now.

"You know, if you're going to take your time, maybe I'll have to do the same with Corinne. Cut off her eyelids first so she can see everything I'm about to do to her. Then again, she's plenty old enough. Maybe I'll just sell her to the Pain & Pleasure House. They always have a need for fresh virgin meat, " Darla mused, a sick edge to her tone that made me want to vomit, if only there was anything in my stomach to allow it. Why was she torturing me like this? I was doing everything she asked me to do.

"Stop! I'm already out. I'm getting to the stairs now. Where do you want me to . . . *Gardax?*" My voice cracked, and I almost dropped the phone. My breath caught in my throat and I was paralyzed.

He was at the bottom of the stairwell, flanked by two burly guys that I assumed must be his security because there could be no other explanation for their flashy body armor plates and the weapons in their hands. Their faces were stoic and somber. Their fists were clenched at their sides.

"*Get out of there!* So help me, she will die, Amy, she *will die.* Do you understand?!" Darla screeched. Her tone was desperate as she cried into the receiver.

Confused and raw, I stepped back, but not soon enough.

Gardax looked up, and our eyes met, hitting me with a mix of emotions. Chief among them, panic. I was torn between running directly for him or charging away like a thief in the night. Gut-wrenching conflict ailed me and robbed my thoughts of anything more than a murky haze.

"Amy!" he called out, but I was already running, my boots slapping the thin boards of the hallway. I drew in narrow breaths. I was afraid to glance over my shoulder for fear of what I would see.

The sound of thunder rocked the stairwell and I knew they were close behind me. There was no way out. Darla was in my ear, hurling horrible threat after threat, and I had the sickening, horrible feeling that I'd just run out of time. This was it. Corinne would be lost to me. I felt pulled in a million directions and I didn't even have a fathom of an idea what kind of danger might befall me, no matter what decision I made. Corinne. I could only think of Corinne and her safety.

Blood screamed in my ears and sweat beaded on my forehead as my breath slowed. I couldn't lose her.

And then I saw it—the waste chute. It was my only resolution, the only escape.

Every floor had one. Residents tossed their refuse down it for compacting and removal. If I could fit inside and slide my way down, I'd narrowly make my escape.

I didn't think, I just ran, pumping everything I had into my legs, and in one swift motion, I tucked my body into one long line and dove down. I didn't know what would happen next, but I was out of options.

"*Nooo!*" I heard Gardax scream behind me, the sound

of his voice doing strange things to me that I didn't have time to examine as I hurtled down the metal tunnel. Why was he so panicked? His screams of agony made my blood turn to icicles inside me.

With a painful thud, I landed in the foul-smelling container at the bottom. I retched and swam my way through the ocean of trash and waste from other refugees' dumpsters.

I scrambled to my feet, searching frantically for the phone that had slipped out of my hands, and then jumped out of the pile of trash. My boots hit the hard concrete floor and I started running for the door.

"I got away," I huffed into the phone.

There was no sound, no answer. Only silence. Where the hell was she now? My emotions were swirling in turmoil, wreaking havoc in my mind.

"*No!* You can't do this, Darla!" I screamed into the phone, panic seizing me once more. I continued to run. The air burned my throat, but I pressed on. I didn't stop. I wouldn't stop until I had confirmation that my sister was unharmed.

I'd just tumbled down five stories of metal tubing, my body doubtlessly bruised and battered in ways my adrenaline was blocking for now. I would feel the pain later. The bruises would be the lasting effects of this whirlwind nightmare.

"I did what you said!" I shouted, more desperate. "Darla! Damn it, answer me!" My tone was angry.

"Cool your twat, I'm still here. Where are you now?" she asked, more casually now, as if she were asking for a prediction on the weather.

My heart beat again. "I'm in the basement. I jumped into the trash chute." I scanned the area, nervously pacing and running a shaky hand through my braid.

"Well, that's where you belong. So fitting. Good, now get out of there. They're not going to give up that easily." Her tone was bitter and mocking.

I nodded silently, catching my breath and running up the steps, breaking through the street access door. I pulled the hood of my coat up, but my hair was wild and loose and fluttered around the sides.

I'd made it less than a dozen paces before I heard him again. "Stop! Amy, wait!" He wailed with enough passionate desperation that I had to turn back and look at him.

I glanced over my shoulder to see him behind me, hot air puffing out of him in a cloud of vapor. His expression was pained and confused.

"You'd better run, trash. Run for your life. Oh, silly me, I mean your sister's," Darla taunted with a sinister chuckle that made me gasp.

I ducked between a couple walking down the path. Horribly as my morning was going, there was some luck to be had. Crowds were beginning to stream onto the sidewalks as people set off for their jobs, starting the business of the day. I could get lost in the shuffle.

I heard him shouting something to his guards, and from the sounds of people being pushed out of the way, I knew he wasn't giving up. We would cause a scene, especially if it looked like I was being chased by the prince.

Sick as it sounds, part of me wanted him to catch me. But a bigger part knew I couldn't let that happen. Darla would make sure I paid the price for that.

I ran into the road, diving between peddlers and vehicles, nearly getting mowed down in the process. I bumped into people, barreled into others. I couldn't stop, no matter how many hiccups I encountered along the way.

Tires squealed and brakes cried out as motorists swerved and stopped to avoid me. A mirror from a passing track smacked against my bag and the force of it knocked me down to the sidewalk where my knees pounded with a brutal thud. My sensitive skin burned in the area where I had landed. I winced in pain, but I had to stand up again and press forward once again.

People craned to see what was going on, but I couldn't stop. I made a run for the alley, hoping to lose him in the moving crowds. I didn't look back anymore. I remained focused on the road in front of me.

Dirty water splashed my boots as I raced down the alley and around a corner, knocking various trash and debris in the process. I ducked and dodged every obstacle in my way, sustaining minor injuries as I went.

"Where are you goin' in such a hurry, pretty baby?" A man caught me by the waist and pulled me toward him, his putrid breath assaulting my senses as he made to kiss me. I grimaced and braced for impact, but I was able to free myself in time before his slimy lips contacted mine.

We struggled briefly while I still held the phone, the sound of Darla's sadistic laughter echoing from the phone's speaker. I'd almost forgotten that I was still connected to her on the line.

"Release her!" I heard Gardax roar from down the alley. His voice was booming and threatening as it crashed through the frigid air.

The man was stunned just enough to give me time to push away and sink a fist into the soft flesh of his gut, right beneath his ribs. He doubled over and released me. I'd lived on the streets for long enough to know how to deal with sleazy guys like that and defend myself.

As soon as I was free, I sprinted again. My lungs seized for oxygen, my muscles ached, but still, I ran. I was running for Corinne's life, not mine. Her life was far more valuable than my own.

Making my way to the other end of the alley, I scrambled over the metal netting of a fence. If I could get two more blocks, I'd be at the transit center, my best chance for losing Gardax. There would be enough warm bodies shuffling about there to help me get lost in the crowd.

"Excuse me, sorry," I tried to manage as I ran through the growing mass of bodies, knocking people down and sending one woman's bag sprawling.

"Watch it, ref-rat!" someone called out, using the derogatory term for homeless refugees.

The dinging sound of the transit center hit me, and I

surged forward, fighting the crowds of night-shift workers making their way toward their homes, leaping over vendor carts and weaving quickly through the churning maze of bodies. I was gasping for air now, red in the face and hair all askew.

I jumped off the sidewalk, into the shoulder of the roadway between the sidewalk and the street, trying to get through the crowd faster. I was surprised at how limber and agile I could make myself as I pushed against the current of people from all angles.

"Out of the way, red!" A cyclist called out, elbowing me as he rode past. His face was puffy in frustration.

The thrust connected with my side and sent me stumbling against the curb. The wind was knocked out of me for a brief moment. I scrambled to get up a second later.

I didn't feel the phone leave my hand, just heard the terrifying splash and crack as it fell into the puddle, the screen shattering. I was powerless to stop it from happening. The damage had been done.

"Nooooooo!" I screamed, the veins in my face feeling like they might explode. I wanted to pass out, to scream and to throw myself on the ground and pound my fists into the pavement, all at once.

On my hands and knees, I reached for it, frantically

trying to wipe the water off it. With fumbling, desperate hands, I prayed that the device would still work.

"Amy." I heard Gardax's voice behind me, but I was too distracted, too devastated to react. I stared at the phone as if it were my only option for ever seeing Corinne again.

"Hello? Hello!" I called, gripped by the temporary hysteria. I screamed into the phone, begging Darla to respond.

The call was disconnected, the phone dead. That was it. I had no other way of contacting Darla. My situation had just gone from hopeless to subliminally dreadful.

I don't remember crying, but I struggled to wipe the water off the phone in vain as I realized the moisture was my own tears splashing down on it. My shoulders shook with regretful sobs that ravaged my body.

A hand on my shoulder shook me out of my breakdown. It was warm and powerful and made me feel instantly safe.

"Amy, please, tell me what's going on?" Gardax asked, crouching in front of me. His eyes displayed genuine concern, flickering with mercy.

His hand felt so warm, his eyes so soft and unsure. I wanted to collapse against him and fall apart. For a minute, I just stared into his eyes, trying to focus my vision. I was breathing hard, my mind racing. The exertion of the chase had left me lightheaded and slightly faint. I wanted to trust him, but I didn't even trust myself in this mindset. There were too many unresolved factors here. I couldn't lean on anyone but myself.

"Please. What's happening? What's wrong?" he begged. He rubbed my back.

But I shook my head, clinging to the one thread of hope I had left. I couldn't tell him anything. Not if I ever wanted to see Corinne again.

"I can't," I breathed. "I can't or my sister will die." Fresh sobs pelted me. The flood of tears wouldn't stop this time. My vision blurred, and the hot tears stung my swollen eyes.

The words seemed to stun him. He opened his mouth to speak, but his eyes were wide with shock and bewilderment and he was momentarily speechless. I could tell by his reaction that he never expected that kind of explanation from me, not in a million years.

An express trolley from the transit dinged, coming

down the street swiftly. It was my only chance. I jumped up and darted toward it, leaping onto the outside handle and clinging with all the strength I had to the massive vehicle as it sped away. As much as I wanted to stay and surrender to Gardax's warmth, I had to rip myself away and disconnect.

Gardax leapt to his feet but he was too late. He wasn't able to jump on in time. In an instant, I was gone.

CHAPTER 13

GARDAX

"Wait!" I cried out again, desperate. I barreled through the people blocking my path, trying to catch the trolley Amy had just thrown herself at. I couldn't lose her, not again. I had too many unanswered questions.

My throat constricted as I fearfully watched her slim body holding to the large vehicle as it zoomed through traffic. I couldn't believe she'd managed to launch herself onto the train with such agility and speed.

I didn't know what was happening, but I knew with crystal-clear conviction that I needed to get to her. I heard Coel's voice somewhere behind me, but I couldn't slow and wait for him. I couldn't stop searching after Amy. I had to find her. Perseverance surged through me with a burst of adrenaline.

I reached a corner and nearly dashed toward Amy, but as I stepped into the street, another trolley passed going the opposite direction, barely missing me. I had to lurch out of the way to keep from smacking directly into the moving train.

The last thing I saw was her long fiery hair billowing freely like some kind of beacon in this dreary gray jungle. A beacon that I lost and desperately needed to find. Frustration rippled through my veins. My knees swayed but didn't completely buckle.

By the time the trolley passed, I had lost sight of her. I struck out, hitting the side of a vendor's cart, denting the thin metal.

"What the hell, man?" The vendor cried out.

"My apologies," I muttered, tossing a generous handful of Union coins on his cart.

His smile grew wide and the animosity melted instantly. "No worries, s'all good, s'all good." He tipped his hat to me.

"Do you have any idea where that trolley that just came through goes?" I asked, taking advantage of his softened attitude and wanting to catch him before he was gone.

He looked in the direction I pointed. "The Express? Manhattan to Central Transit, probably. Most of these lines go there and then branch out to the other boroughs or beyond."

So she could be anywhere. She could have jumped off at any of the locations in between.

"Where'd she go?" Coel asked, reaching me at last.

I looked up to the sky, cursing the situation and myself for being bested. Looking at her, I would never have guessed her capable of such agility and speed. She was driving me half-mad but I still couldn't help but to be impressed. She was like a ninja in the night, mysterious and elusive, and it was a major turn on.

"I don't know," I admitted. "She jumped onto a trolley headed for the main transit hub and I couldn't catch up." I pointed abstractly in the direction she had gone. My senses were now skewed.

He quirked a brow. "*You?* She lost *you?*" He stared at me as if that were the most unimaginable concept ever conjured.

"Yes," I answered darkly. "But not for good. This isn't

over. I still want answers." I narrowed my eyes as I stared into oblivion and the sea of people around me.

As Nur, the other guardsman with us, arrived, we headed back, trying to avoid the shocked stares and gawking pedestrians we passed along the way. It was one thing that I was a prince from a neighboring planet, but it was another that I'd just chased down a refugee civilian.

"Isn't that the—"

"Holy shit! That's one of those aliens!"

"Quick, take a picture!"

We hurried through the growing attention and made it back to our vehicle. I climbed in, frustrated and annoyed at the gawking stares and unflattering terms shot at me by the whispering pedestrians.

"Well, shall we return to the ship?" Nur asked, punching commands into the control panel. His nonchalance was infuriating me. I still had a job to do. I wouldn't rest until Amy was safely in my presence.

"No, we're going to Manhattan," I ordered, belting out the instructions as if there was no room for debate on the subject.

Coel looked at me curiously. "You think we can beat

her there?" I didn't know if it was a challenge or a dare, but I was up to accepting either way.

I shook my head. "No, but she said something before I lost her. I asked her what was going on and she refused to tell me. Her sister's life is at stake. Something is very wrong with this situation and I suspect we will need the assistance of the human authorities." My voice was shakier than I intended, but the situation was dire.

"Perhaps it would be better that I handle the matter for you, Your Highness. If the girl is in danger, as she says, your involvement may place you in harm's way." Coel was always looking out for my best interest. I had to respect him for his efforts to subdue me.

"I understand your concern and I appreciate it, but I'm going to see this through. I suspect her involvement with me is what has put her at risk, and I'll not sit idly by, hoping for the best," I affirmed. Nothing would change my mind.

"But—"

I leveled him with a glare, not meaning to vent my frustration but finding it difficult to remain unaffected by the events of the morning.

"What would you do, Coel? If it was Yezia?"

His eyes narrowed, jaw clenched. "I'd rip apart anyone who threatened her."

"Then you'll understand," I said with a curt nod.

He didn't argue, and we headed for Union Hall in silence with determination, full-steam ahead.

AT THIS LOW ALTITUDE AND IN THE BRIGHTNESS OF daylight, it was much easier to make out the human establishments which had been little more than homogenous, distant figures. Up close, I found myself quite admiring the beauty of their architecture. It was chaotic and gritty, but somehow, oddly beautiful. It was something unique to the area and unlike anything one would find on my home planet.

We reached the roof of the Union Hall, which I had visited only once before upon our arrival here on Earth. My heart raced in anticipation and excitement with the bewildered hope of finding Amy somewhere around the area.

Coel had notified the authorities ahead of our arrival and we were greeted by a woman in a simple black jumpsuit.

"Prince Gardax, please follow me," she said, turning

around and walking toward the rooftop entrance. Her lips were flatlined and her expressionless features gave little away of her thoughts on the matter.

We climbed into an elevator and descended several levels before being led down a dimly lit hallway and a series of staff offices before finally arriving in a well-accommodated lobby.

"The mayor will be with you shortly," she informed us and then walked away.

I was unimpressed with their diplomatic hospitality thus far. After a considerable amount of time had passed, I grew impatient and approached the young man seated at the desk outside what was clearly the main office. As I approached, the door finally swung open and a heavyset person of ambiguous gender nodded. I needed answers and was prepared to demand them.

"Prince Gardax, welcome. I'm Mayor Schrute. Please come in." He gave me an apprehensive, albeit polite, grin.

With Coel and Nur at my side, we entered and stood before the desk which was backed by a wall of windows that looked out onto a massive green space. I wondered whether this was the 'Central Park' I'd heard about.

"I understand that you are looking for someone? A citizen of the Union, correct?" The mayor stroked a small furry creature on the desk. He appeared bored and uninterested.

"Yes, a member of my staff. I have reason to believe she and her sister are in imminent danger. I require your assistance in tracking her. Her name is Amy," I began.

"I'm sorry, but you'll have to back up. Do you have any evidence of a threat? Any reason I should concern myself with your staffing issues?" the mayor asked, somewhat condescendingly. He made brief eye contact with me before looking away.

"I have her word that her sister's life was in danger," I answered. I didn't know what else he wanted from me as far as an explanation went. Threats to human life should be valued by these humans.

With a dry laugh, the mayor answered, "I'm afraid that's not quite enough. People's lives are in danger all the time in New York. That is hardly newsworthy. It's a harsh world here. I'll need a little more to go on if you think we're going to launch some kind of investigative operation." He behaved as if the safety of Amy and her sister was none of his concern.

I squared my jaw and clenched my sweaty fists. I

almost shouted, but Coel eyed the mayor shrewdly, and reaching into the space between his armor and his clothing, he pulled out a slim satchel, dropping it on the Mayor's desk.

I watched as, with a flicker of excitement, the mayor reached out and opened the packet. "We'll call this the first payment. With another to come once we find her." He'd quickly begun to whistle a different tune once money was involved.

Annoyed and relieved at once, I nodded. "Thank you," I mumbled and swiftly smiled at Coel.

"Now, I'll need to know her Citizen ID number." The mayor began listing a set of requirements. I gave what information I could with a promise to send the rest as soon as possible.

We were led back to our transport once more and headed back to my ship to gather the remaining information. Time was of the essence right now, with not a second left to waste.

"The Mayor's office assures us they'll find her within the next week," Coel informed me.

"A *week?*" I fumed. "Surely, they can do better!" I'd given him a sizable sum of money. I expected more.

Sympathy showed in his eyes, but Coel shook his

head. "I offered double the bounty, but they assured me there was no way they could speed the matter any further."

I sat back, raking my hands through my hair in frustration. "I don't like this." I shook my head and blew out a puff of ragged air.

"Nor I, but without their resources, our chances of finding her on our own are slim." Coel always spoke the truth, even if it hurt.

"Very well, keep me informed of any developments." I nodded, dismissing Coel because I was too tormented to keep up a conversation.

Left to my own solitude, I paced. I tried to distract myself with business from home. I did everything I could to wear my body and mind down enough that I wasn't racked with worry over her.

But still, in my mind, I saw the fear and the desperation in her eyes. Something was very, very wrong and there was nothing I could do about it until I found her and begged her to come clean with the issues that plagued and threatened her.

I watched the lights below, as if I expected her to come floating up toward me through the night air, until my eyelids grew heavy.

And then she was there.

Standing before me, just as I'd seen her that morning, her long hair loose in soft and silky waves falling around the perfect angles of her face, her slender shoulders. I breathed a sigh of relief, mesmerized by the way she gently floated to me like a perfect dream of a woman.

"Amy?" I asked, and she came to me without question, without running.

"You found me," she whispered, smiling with devilish features curling at the edges of her lips.

I fell to my knees, overcome with relief. "I was so worried. I thought I'd lost you. I thought someone was after you or that you'd been harmed because of me."

"Shh," she assured me. "It's okay. I'm here with you now. I survived and we're together. That's what counts." Her voice was like a song, silky and smooth and a paradise to my ears.

I nodded, standing and raising her hands to my lips. The scent of her skin reached me, far more potent than any Tora pollen Rawklix might distill. I was intoxicated by her gaze, by her slender body in front of me.

Before I realized what I was doing, I was pulling her toward me, cradling her scalp in my hands and kissing her, her hair tangling in my fingers, tasting the sweetness of her as my body ignited with the heated awareness of hers. Her breath was both icy and hot on my skin, a perfect combination.

Her strong, finely boned hands snaked around my neck. "Now that you've found me, what are you going to do with me?" she asked, her voice a seductive tease that sent a shiver of arousal through me.

"Everything," I said, and she smiled, blushing slightly. The sky was the limit. She was mine to explore.

"Show me," she answered, stepping back and lifting the hem of her long tunic up and over her head, exposing her naked body to my appreciative gaze. I couldn't stop staring at her creamy smooth skin. She was stunning.

I growled some form of inaudible response and pressed against her, her back to the transparent glass wall, the lights of the city below us like they shone for us alone. Rabid and hungry, she peeled the clothes off me, freeing my erection and enclosing it in the warm silk of her palm. My breath caught when she placed her lips along my length. The sight of her naked before me was too erotic, too intense.

I pulled her up, needing to taste her as well, and feasted at the exposed flesh of her firm, rounded breasts, and the sound of her sigh, breathy and delicate, burned me. I lifted her legs, wrapping them around my hips, settling her to straddle me. I could feel the wet heat of her pressed against my hard shaft and I knew she was as eager and ready as I was.

I drove into her, her tight passage closing around me, pulling me deeper into her, as she clung to my shoulders, her nails biting my flesh with every thrust. She moaned softly, quietly through my pulsing ears.

The little sounds she made grew more and more urgent and placed me in her thrall. I lived only to hear the pleasure in her voice, to feel the growing tremble of her flesh around mine as she came for me. We rocked back and forth together with rhythmic, fluid movements that united our chemistry.

Driven to the brink, I sank into her one more time, the chill of the glass behind her on my arms contrasting from the explosion that rocked through me as I lost myself. An explosion of ecstasy blinded me as I groaned with passionate fury.

Finding my breath, I carried her to the bed, collapsing into the soft cushions with her.

I closed my eyes and smiled, finally feeling at peace.

My thirst had been quenched, at least for now. I knew it was only a matter of time before I craved her with desperate hunger once again.

"Is that smile for me?" she asked, her voice raspy from our lovemaking. Her cheeks were still flushed, glowing in the aftermath.

I opened my eyes, reaching out for her.

But she wasn't there.

The room was dark with no sign of Amy. I was alone. Alone and haunted. The dream was a fog that lifted as soon as reality came crashing down on me.

CHAPTER 14

AMY

I t was still dark when I woke up. The cold winds that tore through my thin coat gave me no reprieve and I needed to be out of here before people started to trickle through. To be honest, I was surprised when I opened my eyes and realized that I was still alive, enduring a night in horrendously frigid conditions.

I'd slept under a bush beside the icy waters of the Hudson River to avoid detection, and my body was stiff and aching everywhere. I was on the Jersey side, where I knew Darla and her husband lived. Beyond the city, I had no idea where to find her, but it felt like a place to start. If I could keep convincing myself that I was one step closer with every move I made, then that was all the hope I needed to cling to.

I pulled my coat around me, climbing the railing and jogging along the path to keep warm until I got to a roadway. The sun was starting to lighten the sky and traffic was picking up. Soon, sleepy people would begin to drag themselves out of bed and the hustle of the world would awaken under the dawn of a new day. I bought a hot bagel and lox from a sidewalk vendor, sparing one of the few precious coins I had left.

After the exertions of the day before, I knew I needed to fortify myself, even if it meant making myself a little poorer. The lox was a rare treat and I savored it for as long as I possibly could. I knew I wouldn't have a meal like that again for a while.

A pang of guilt struck me as I wondered what Corinne was eating . . . if Darla was even still feeding her. I tried to justify the guilty pleasure with the fact that I needed strength and energy if I was ever going to make it to the finish line of finding Corinne.

I walked the streets, pulling my hood low over my face and sweeping my hair under the collar of my coat, doing what I could to blend into the mass of people. But I was walking aimlessly, without direction. The chance of coming across Darla was ridiculous, but it was all I had. Sometimes, miracles happened at random.

I needed a plan, though, in case fate didn't bring me one of those lucky breaks.

I couldn't go home. Darla was clear about that. But I certainly wasn't going to abide by her conditions until I knew Corinne was safe, unharmed. I couldn't just continue to live outside and sleep in bushes.

I had to think things through. What did I know? I knew Darla didn't want me around the prince, so going to her on the ship wouldn't work. I knew if I went to the authorities or Gardax, Darla would hurt Corinne before they got to her, so that wasn't an option. The only way I was going to get Corinne back was to assure Darla that I hadn't broken any of her instructions. It seemed like she had a constant watchful eye on me, and there was no escaping her wrath.

The phone was busted though. I pulled it out of my pocket and tapped it a little too roughly. A piece of glass chipped off and fell to the ground. Not a good sign so far.

But maybe the damage was just external. If I could find a tech ravager, maybe I could pull some data out of it. I jogged over to a bodega, asking for directions to the nearest e-scrapper.

The owner, a thin man with eyes that bugged out

beneath a pair of caterpillar-thick eyebrows, looked down at me over the rim of his glasses and silently pointed up.

"What floor?" I asked.

He held up three fingers and then returned his attention back to his paper as if I had vanished. I turned to walk away but the front page caught my attention and I halted in my tracks and stared at the print screaming across the page as well as the picture rocking my core.

It was Gardax and his brothers. They were announcing another ball to be held once more at his ship. The thought of him surrounded by hordes of eager, beautiful women unsettled me, but I closed my eyes against the rush of feeling. I needed to focus. I guess he'd forgotten about me even after the scuffle yesterday. Perhaps he'd given up. That idea both crushed me and relieved me.

I'd nearly broken down the day before. I was lucky I'd been delirious, because I'm not sure I would have been able to run from him otherwise. Not after the way he'd looked at me. His eyes had been hungry and desperate for answers.

I steeled my jaw as I pushed through the door of the small, rundown brick building. I didn't have time for this kind of emotion. Weakness hadn't gotten me this far, and it certainly wasn't the way to finish this with Darla. She would be able to sniff out any sign of weakness and use it to destroy me.

I needed to be strong for Corinne's sake, for my own, even. If I let myself feel this, it'd be like chipping away at that wall I'd built to protect myself from all the awful things I couldn't afford to dwell on. I catalogued the memory and put it away in its own neat box along with everything else that I was better off forgetting. I just hoped it stayed there. I couldn't afford to unearth those cobwebs.

Jogging up the cold tile steps, I found the third floor and started down the hallway, wondering where the heck the e-scrapper was. Every door looked the same, dark green with faded gold letters and nothing else. There were no names, no titles, nothing. It was bleak and dreary up here. I couldn't imagine what it must be like to report to work in a cold and gloomy place like this.

I couldn't exactly knock on every door, hoping to find the e-scrapper. It was too risky. What if I encountered a predator of some sort? I wasn't going to do anything senseless to cause myself to become the hunted.

Another dead end. I walked back the way I came, but

as I was mentally berating the rude bodega man, a small explosion sounded from the far end of the hall. I instinctively shielded my head with my arms. The wind was knocked out of me, more from shock than anything else.

The dark green door flew open, and a huge man, maybe seven feet tall, came stomping out, red-faced and carrying scraps that were still letting off bright blue sparks of electricity. I cowered in the corner, wanting to make sure to keep myself veiled as much as possible.

"You pay for this, little man! The boss, she not gonna be happy with you!" he said, shouting over his shoulder and pushing past me as if I was a fly to be swatted away, if he'd even noticed me at all.

A scrawny teenager with mocha skin and shocks of bleached hair popped out, char marks on his white thermal. He frantically scrambled up to the giant man.

"Rupo, wait! I can fix it! Just let me try one more time. I just used the wrong converter. It'll be fine, you'll see," he called after the big man in desperation as if every word depended on the response.

I watched as he chased him down to the street. Through the glass window above the door, I could see them arguing before the big man fumed off. I stayed in the same spot, immobilized with curiosity and fear of the unknown.

The teen sagged, shoulders slumped, then sprinted in the building again and straight past me, too distracted by his own turmoil to notice.

"Hey! Wait!" I called out.

"Sorry, can't! There's gonna be some very angry folks back here soon. I suggest you make a run for it too. I wouldn't want to be around here when they get back." His voice cracked on the last of his statement, belying his young age.

"But I need help. My sister could die," I argued, blocking his path. He was even scrawnier looking up close.

He looked up at me, unimpressed. "Yeah? Well, tell her to join the club." The cynical tone was not lost on me. He spoke as if there were no hope left in the world to hold onto.

Our eyes met and his voice trailed off. I blushed under the scrutiny. "What?" I scowled.

"It's you!" he exclaimed with excitement and pointed a mocha-colored bony finger at my chest.

"And you're you, so now we've got that out of the way,

can you help me out? It won't take long." I was confused as I continued to press him.

He hurried past me, grabbing my sleeve and pulling me with him. "Yes, but we gotta hurry."

"Okay." I followed him back to his apartment. It was full of metal racks with various devices and compu-scraps. The entire place was littered with electronics.

As I watched, he ran to the closet and grabbed a small pack before waving me on. Opening a window, he grabbed onto a gutter pipe and slid down to the alley below. Was I really supposed to follow him?

The situation wasn't inspiring much comfort, but it was all I had to go on and he hadn't completely denied me of help yet.

When we were a few blocks away and he'd pulled on a thick stocking cap, popping the color of his jacket, he finally spoke again.

"I'm Bodi, by the way. E-scrapper, savant, jack of all trades, male model, and budding mogul." He grinned proudly with a set of teeth that were pearly white.

"Ok, I'm—"

"You're Amy Allen, from Refugee Precinct 6. I know all about you," he said as if announcing the weather.

His tone was so casual that it made me unsettled. How the hell did he know who I was?

"Excuse me?" I struggled, stammering as I stared at him in shock, mouth agape.

"I got a notice last night from my client network. You are hot cakes right now and my ticket out of this shit hole," he continued. His explanation was vaguer that I cared for it to be, and I needed him to elaborate and get on with the point.

I stopped in my tracks. "Whoa. I'm not going anywhere with you until you explain how the hell you know anything about me." I grabbed him by the crook of his elbow and held him in place, refusing to let go. My grip on him was solid.

He rolled his eyes at my lack of comprehension and brought me up to speed. Gardax had bought the help of some powerful people who Bodi happened to be on the bad side of after he'd hacked their network and gotten caught. He'd had some temporary protection from a local paid posse but that bridge had burned this morning along with the device he was trying to fix for them.

We were on our way to turn me in, he informed me.

I acted reflexively, wrapping him in a choke hold. I gritted my teeth and gave him a death stare.

"The only way you're dragging me in is if I'm unconscious. Like you'll be in about three seconds if I tighten this grip," I warned in a snarly voice. I was stronger than him and it wouldn't be hard to kill him.

"Okay," he croaked as I released him. "Jesus, what's your problem?" he asked, rubbing the skin beneath his jaw where I'd started to cut off his blood supply. He coughed a little for dramatic affect.

"You told me you'd help me. Now are you a scrapper or not?" I raised an eyebrow and pushed myself so close to him that we were only an inch or so apart. He smelled like body odor.

"Dude, a *prince* is looking for you. And you want my help to *avoid* him? I'd be doing you a favor getting you connected. There's some shady folks would ransom you, but I'm not like that. But I do have an ass to cover. Do you know what they're going to do to me if they find out I let you go? Have some humanity, lady. Word gets out we crossed paths and I *didn't* alert the bosses, just toss me in the Hudson now." He raised his arms defensively.

He wasn't much older than Corinne, if I had to guess. Maybe fifteen. From the looks of him and the dilapidated place he'd been scrounging in, I had a feeling he'd been on his own for a while. And damn it, I felt bad for him, remembering how hard that was, what it was like to have no one. He was desperate, and he had a way to escape this decrepit lifestyle. I couldn't blame him, but I couldn't allow him to get his wish granted either.

"All right, I'll make a deal with you. You get me the number I need off this phone, and I'll let you take my picture and send it in. Tell them you've spotted me. That should count for something, right?" I asked in a cheerier voice, aiming to be able to compromise with the little weasel.

Bodi studied me in that wary way I knew well because it was how I viewed other people too. "Okay. But I need a little more. Let me plant a tracker on you, then you ditch it somewhere with something of yours. a jacket or something." It wasn't a terrible idea. I could roll with these punches.

I agreed and explained, in broad strokes, what was going on. He took my phone and examined it. We settled in an alleyway behind a rotten-smelling dumpster, and he pulled out a series of tools from his pack, plugging the phone into a small box and fiddling. Sparks flew for a moment and my heart sank. That wasn't a good sign.

"Got it," he announced, grinning through his safety goggles. I closed my eyes against the relief. "Thank you," I murmured as a prayer song of gratitude.

Darla's number in hand, we walked over to another bodega and I spent a very large portion of my remaining money on a basic burner phone, punching the numbers in. This option was far more important than having food. I could always scrounge in dumpsters to stay alive, but I'd never be lucky enough to stumble upon a burner phone.

It rang and rang, and my nerves ate at me so furiously, I didn't think there'd be much left of me if she didn't answer. I held my breath and waited, a tumbling wreck inside.

"Hello?" Darla's voice finally answered in that fake-nice voice she'd used when we first met. She must be expecting someone else to be on the other end of the receiver. I saw right through her phoniness.

"It's Amy. I did what you said. I got away and the prince knows nothing. Now, tell me, is Corinne okay?" I asked, fear rippling through me as Bodi looked on, pretending not to hear my conversation.

"Well, well, well. Look who is a little lying piece of trash. The prince *does* know something. He knows you didn't just quit, you dumb bitch, and now he's looking for you. For that, and for making me wait twenty-four hours for a fucking call back, you're going to be punished," she said, her voice far too calm. The hairs raised on the back of my neck. Darla's threats got worse every time I spoke to her.

The phone clicked and then heated. I pulled it from my face and the tiny screen lit up with a picture. It was Corinne in some tiny, dark space. She was tied, her skin red and enflamed where the rope cut into her. Somewhere beside me, Bodi gasped, but luckily, he was out of sight of the camera.

My eyes welled with sorrowful tears and pooled over the sides of my cheeks, running down my face and burning me. "Corinne!" I cried. "Corinne, honey, I'm doing everything I can."

"Save it. Your sister knows what a failure you are. And here is her permanent reminder." Her voice was wicked and sinister.

Darla appeared in the shot, blocking Corinne for a moment. Something red glowed in her hand, and when she touched it to Corinne, eliciting a scream of agony, I realized what it was. Darla's voice was raspy and grotesque from years of smoking, and now, I had to watch as she tortured Corinne with one of her godawful cigarettes.

The hot end seared into Corinne's sensitive skin as if it were a branding tool, leaving a permanent mark forever, just like Darla warned. She snickered with amusement, watching my sister writhe in delirious pain. It was a struggle and a nightmare to endure witnessing this terrible act of abuse, even over the phone.

Fat tears rolled down my cheeks as I begged her to stop. After what felt like an eternity, Corinne's shrieks became little more than moans as Darla dotted burn marks up and down her arms. The damage had been done. Corinne whimpered and then went limp and quiet.

"Please, please stop!" I pleaded. I would do anything to take my sister's pain away and bear the burden myself.

Darla turned back to look at me, angling her head to the side with those cold, lifeless eyes of hers. Her stare was like glancing directly into the soul of the devil.

"You want me to stop?" She smiled. "Okay. You're right, this is too easy to cover. Let's make her really remember how you messed up." She pulled a pair of kitchen scissors out and my stomach dropped. The sky was the limit as far as the twisted ways of torture that Darla could inflict on the world.

"Hmm. what should I take?" she said, dragging the pointed end across Corinne's cheek. Looking back, she warned darkly, "Don't fuck up again, Amy." Then she grabbed the bulk of Corinne's hair and lopped it off in one chop. "Next time, it'll be something that doesn't grow back, and when I've finished with her, I'll find you and dissect you like the vermin you are."

Blood trickled down the blades of the scissors and I knew she'd cut Corinne in the process. Corinne didn't flinch. She was probably too numb from the pain or passed out. Her eyes were sealed shut but I could tell that she was still breathing by the way her shoulders raised up and down.

"I'm so sorry, Corinne. I'm . . ." I cried, not having the words to finish. Words held no value anyway. It was action that would take her pain away.

Corinne looked up at me then, her eyes cold and hard, her jaw clenched. "Get the cops and find this bitch."

Darla's hand slapped Corinne's cheek with a painful, sharp whack and the call dropped. I knew that Corinne would probably have to pay for that statement, but I almost smiled when I realized that the little light of survival was still burning within Corinne. She had the vibrance to fight, and as long as she wasn't giving up, neither was I.

It took me a moment to refocus. My hands were

shaking, my vision clouded by tears. My shoulders shook with sobs. I squeezed my eyes shut and prayed to wake up soon from this nightmare.

"Shit. you're in it deep too, huh?" Bodi said, finally breaking the silence, and I looked back at him, nodding as my mind raced. His eyes were curious and careful.

"I'll find you." Darla didn't know where I was. The cheap burner phone couldn't be traced. It was a rare moment of freedom and I seized it. For the first time in this ordeal, I had the upper hand.

I punched in Gardax's number and held my breath, waiting to hear his voice. There would be no Darla waiting to listen in on the call. This realization gave me fervent energy and hopeful enthusiasm.

But he didn't answer. The automated voice on the other line instructed me to leave a message, so I did. I hurried to tell him everything I could fit in a message. It felt like I was ripping open all the carefully maintained boxes in my mind, but I clung to the hope that it would be worth it. I told him how Darla had tricked me into thinking we were friends, then used everything she knew about me to torment me. How she had Corinne and was hurting her to prevent me from reaching out to him.

If the concern in his eyes was sincere, maybe, just maybe, he could help. I prayed that he'd be able to hear the message without it being intercepted by Darla first.

Finally, I drew the phone away and clicked it off, praying that he'd get it, praying that I hadn't just sealed Corinne's death warrant.

"So, what are you gonna do now?" Bodi asked. I'd almost forgotten he was there in my ambitious focus.

I swallowed and recentered. "Right, our deal."

He shook his head. "Nah, it's okay." He lifted his shirt and revealed a crisscross pattern of scars from his hip to his armpit. "We all tryin' to survive, right? Look, I've got a backup place, off the grid. I'm headed there. You can lie low there too, if you want. Safety in numbers, eh?"

And for the first time in as many years as I could remember, I hugged someone other than Corinne. Maybe there were good people left out there in the world after all.

CHAPTER 15

GARDAX

I'd not rested easy, and when I woke, it barely registered. The whole night had been little more than a waking dream. Amy intruded into every thought, every dream. My sleep had been restless, and my eyes burned with fatigue.

"Rise and shine, brother," Darbnix's voice reached my ears, so deep it sounded almost artificial.

I sat up and looked toward the direction of his voice. Through the sheer, iridescent curtains of my bed, I could see him lounging in a chair, staring out at the view below.

"A fascinating planet, is it not?" he murmured. "Such lush natural environments and yet the populace hide themselves away in these massive concrete hives, as if they are afraid of the planet that gives them life."

Darbnix was most at home in the wild, which suited him well to his province of Noor, where the bulk of Trilynia's food and sustenance came from. "I have acquired a number of interesting plant and animal specimens for our eventual return, though. I've quite enjoyed my excursions into the wilderness here."

"I wouldn't know. Coel doesn't allow me off the ship much," I grumbled. He was speaking in such a pacifying, trance-like lull that it angered and frustrated me. Didn't he know what a nervous wreck I was about this whole Amy situation?

Darbnix chuckled. "The costs of being the eldest, I suppose. You're too precious and delicate to risk." His voice was only slightly resentful, but I felt the barb anyway.

"Hmph. Step into the training module with me and I'll show you just how *delicate*," I argued.

He laughed again. "No doubt. Listen, I've heard reports that you may have found your bride. Is it true?" He glanced over at me for the first time since he began talking.

I shrugged into a robe and walked to the transparent

wall. "I suspect as much, but I can't know until I've scanned her, which is proving problematic."

"Left that good of an impression on her?" he teased, but it stung.

I scrubbed the sleep from my face, sighing. "I don't know. But she certainly left an impression on me. I can barely pass a few moments without thinking of her, worrying where she might be. She's in danger of some kind, but she couldn't or wouldn't trust me." I looked back at him. "I don't like being helpless."

Darbnix nodded. "No, I imagine you would not. Is there anything I can do?" A purple watch lizard jumped from his pocket and onto his shoulder as he stood and walked toward me. Those damn things were so annoying, and he never left home without one slinking by his side.

I shook my head and bade Vesper to bring up Amy's file, allowing Darbnix to glance through her information. "We've enlisted the help of the human authorities, however they're slow and bogged down by bureaucracy. Coel tells me that the best we can do is wait, but I'd much rather be doing *something,* even if it is just walking the streets looking for her," I explained. I couldn't sit idly by, fretting while waiting for people to do something I felt like I might have a capability of performing myself.

"She has a pretty strength to her," he nodded, skimming. "As for Coel, he has your best interest in mind, Brother. Jokes aside, you truly are too important to our people to risk." He shook his head as if it pained him to admit that fact.

I threw him a dubious expression. "Yes, it's not like I have any siblings who could assume my role if something should happen to me." My tone was frisky, yet sardonic.

He laughed. "I don't think so. Better you than me. I don't have a taste for the glitz of the capital. I'm much happier working the land, making myself useful. Erebis is yours to keep. As for your woman, I make frequent trips to the surface and I've made some contacts. I'll look into things, see if I can assist." His smile and tone were both genuine.

"I'd never turn down the offer. Thank you, Brother," I said, clasping hands.

"By the way, can you point me in the direction of your researcher's offices?" He asked, reaching into his pocket and pulling his scanner out. It was scratched and looked to have sustained massive abuse.

"What did you do? Hurl it in a volcano?" I couldn't help but bellow with laughter. So it appeared as if I wasn't the only one having issues with the fragility of the device.

He smiled sheepishly. "My pets got curious." He shrugged. The lizard on his shoulder leapt at the scanner, and he pulled it off, grasping it firmly by the tail. "No! Leave it," he said firmly. "I don't want them to make it worse," he groaned with frustration.

I nodded and told him where to find Lifiya's lab. We parted ways, and I focused on the business of the day. There was a lot to conquer, and I had to find a leaping-off point.

Darbnix and my brothers were all on the ship, or would be shortly, in preparation for the ball the following night. We were hosting another soiree, this one even more grand than the last. I could do nothing but dread it. What was the point? I couldn't get Amy out of my mind long enough to look at another woman, and even if I could socialize with guests, I knew none of them were my bride, so the whole affair felt pointless. Everything seemed superficial and trivial. If Amy's life was in danger, I felt guilty about leaving her in the shadows while I entertained dinner guests I cared nothing about.

But I must not think only of myself. My brothers had not gotten any closer to identifying mates, and I needed to keep them on task, unlike the last party where they, most of them, anyway, spent the occasion practicing their charms on their eager attendants, even after negative readings disqualified them from the possibility of being matches. I wasn't the only one looking for a mate, and I couldn't assume a selfish attitude on the subject.

This was not going to be another night of idle pleasure spent flirting. I would make sure of that. We had a job to do. We were on a mission driven by genetic ingenuity and desperation. The future of our entire race depended on our success with finding fertile Earth mates. I missed my home and yearned to eventually go back, hopefully, with Amy by my side.

I got dressed, getting ready to head to the ballroom to check on the preparations for the party. I glanced at my human phone on the shelf outside my training module. The screen was lit, and when I grabbed it, it stated that I had a message. Hoping that the mayor's office might have some news for me, I started to unlock the message when Coel's voice came from the door, announcing himself and requesting entrance.

Eagerly, I turned to him, assuming he must have the latest intel to relay. Instead, his expression was apologetic.

"Your Highness, Mrs. Barnaby, the catering supervisor, has requested an audience with you."

I rolled my eyes, but before I could dismiss the notion or tell him I was busy, she stepped into the room. "Oh, Your Highness!" she said, sweeping into a curtsy. Great. I couldn't muster up an excuse to escape her if she was standing right in front of me.

She was dressed in civilian clothes rather than her work attire. The fabric clung to her in indecent ways that seemed entirely out of place for an interview with your employer, not to mention at such an early hour. She was a married woman, but she certainly wasn't playing the role of a doting and trustworthy spouse in the absence of her husband.

I trained my eyes on her face, forcing a tight, polite smile. "Can I help you, Mrs. Barnaby? Is something wrong with the catering preparations?"

"Actually, it's just *Ms.* Barnaby now," she corrected with a winking smile that gave me chills.

Coel cleared his throat and excused himself. Wretched man.

"Oh, my apologies," I answered formally and indifferently.

She stepped forward, swaying her hips in too obvious a fashion as she moved. "Thank you, but I'm not. Our marriage died a long time ago." Her voice was a whisper and eerily portrayed desperate seduction.

"Oh," I said awkwardly and shifted my weight, clearing my throat and looking anywhere and everywhere besides her.

"Call me Darla, please," she said, smiling as she reached me. Her tongue slithered aggressively out of her mouth as if she were waiting for me to pounce and kiss her or something.

"Well, Darla, I must say this is highly irregular. Is there something you wanted? As you know, we're hosting a party tomorrow and I must attend to the arrangements." I waved her off dismissively, but she failed to exit, the message going right over her head.

She looked up at me through her lashes, angling her head to the side. Something about her eyes seemed cold, I thought, irregular and void of emotion. She was almost robotic.

"Your Highness. Gardax," she said, though I hadn't given her leave to call me by my name. "I hope I don't sound too forward, but I just feel such a strong pull between us, a connection I can't fight anymore. Surely, you must feel it too?" Her perfume burned as it filled my nostrils. Had she tried to drown herself in the stuff?

I opened my mouth to deny it, but she pressed on. "I know you have a world of women to choose from, but

I could never live with myself if I didn't speak now, if I let this pass us by because I was too shy to speak out." She continued to bat her eyelashes in that sickening way.

The way she was leaning into me felt quite the opposite of shy. She was contradicting herself and pretending to be someone she wasn't, a detestable act and something that annoyed me.

"I have come to you this morning to humbly submit myself to be scanned. I know you've scanned others in the kitchen and I think I know why you've waited to scan me. It's because you feel it too, this power between us, and it wasn't right, not while I was married. But you don't have to be afraid anymore. I'm not."

I wanted to politely but firmly decline the offer, but I stopped short of doing so. What could it hurt to scan her and be done with these uncomfortable interactions? It was clear she had set her sights on such a match, so it was only right that she should have her disappointment and be allowed to move on. For God's sake, the woman had left her husband on this wild notion! I hated to be the bearer of bad news for her, but the quicker we got this uncomfortable interaction over with, the better for both of us.

"Ms. Barnaby, or Darla, rather, you are right. I

should have scanned you. Allow me to quickly rectify that," I said, pulling the scanner out and turning it on.

As the device activated and hummed to life, I felt a stab of apprehension but quickly disregarded it. It would be like ripping off a Band-Aid. Surely, she wouldn't be my match.

Holding the scanner out between us, partially in an effort to force her to back up as she was entirely too close, I gave her an apologetic expression as it didn't react. To my relief. The scanner remained still and quiet, void of any interaction.

But then, to my horror, it did. All of a sudden, out of nowhere, my worst nightmare began to flash and hum right in front of my eyes. I was powerless to stop it. I jerked the scanner and slapped on it, certain that there was some sort of mistake.

It began to vibrate and light up. It flickered for a moment then slowly began growing brighter and brighter. My stomach dropped and the room seemed to go out of focus as the awful reality slammed into my brain.

Darla's expression was somehow calm and satisfied, despite my inability to mask my own shock or displeasure. Her lips were curled into a sinister and satisfied grin. The smirk and smugness on her face made me roar inside with fury.

The scanner finally emitted a series of clicks, and a report appeared on the screen, listing the results of the reading and summarily declaring her my mate. This couldn't be happening to me. I was shrinking into the abyss of despair. The walls were closing in, threatening to swallow me whole.

Her. Darla. My mate. My biological mate. My genetic match. How was this possible?

It couldn't be. It defied explanation. How could I be so repulsed by the person most suited for me? I needed answers. I wouldn't rest or accept this as my fate until I had the solid evidence and proof to back this assessment up with scientific steel.

"Oh, Gardax!" she said, throwing herself at me and planting an unwanted kiss on my cheek as I fortunately turned just in time for her to miss my mouth. Her sloppy return landed on my cheek. I tried not to visibly look appalled as I tried to free myself from her grasp.

I scrambled back, extracting myself from her grasp and knocking over a breakfast tray that rested on the table beside me. Dishes shattered and metal clattered against the floor. Food splattered against the walls.

Coel came running in. "Prince Gardax! Are you well?"

I slumped back, staring blankly, unable to form words. My mind was still in shock.

"We've matched!" Darla announced, turning to Coel and grabbing the scanner out of my hands to show off the evidence. "I suppose that makes me your boss now." She smiled with a cold satisfaction that made my skin crawl. Was she already spinning devious webs to gain power?

Coel looked from her to the scanner and then to me. "Your Highness?" His frown and furrowed brow gave way that he thought this must be some kind of terrible joke.

I looked up at him, dumbfounded. "It's true," I managed to croak out, wildly numb and tingly with disappointment. The world moved in slow motion. I couldn't contain a single calculated thought.

My life descended into a depressing chaos. Darla burst into a flurry of activity, demanding that we make an announcement and ordering accommodations to be arranged for her on the ship. She was bouncing around the room like a wasp, buzzing from order to order.

Ironically, she seemed far less interested in interacting with me now that the scanner had declared her my bride and far more content to lord over the servants and staff. She spoke in a sadistic and assertive tone, waving her hands animatedly in the air as she barked orders left and right.

This could not be my life. Could it? Could I resign myself to marriage with someone I could barely stand to be in the same room with? I racked my brain, trying to find some link or similarity between us that could justify the pairing.

But there was simply a total absence of reason or logic. Nothing made sense. Chaos and reality blended into one harsh, beaming ray of despair.

My thoughts went back to Rawklix's comments, not so long ago, about obeying the rule of the scanner, even if it matched us with a warty pit-dweller, as he'd so tactfully put it. Was he right? It seemed like a vicious joke that would never come true back then, but now, I was facing the beast with no way out.

The notion that I could be matched with someone to whom I was not at all attracted had been a possibility, but now I was faced with the certainty of it. It was one thing to not be entertained by an aesthetically pleasing person, but it was another to loathe your mate altogether.

I had the better part of the day to come to grips with it before Darbnix sought me out.

"Well, those human authorities are faster than you gave them credit for! I understand you've matched. Congratulations!" he said with a hearty smile on his face. He gave me a fond pat on the back. His hand landed on my skin with a brotherly smack.

I looked at him, numb and distracted. "No. it's not her. It was someone else, a catering supervisor on the ship." My voice sounded cloudy and distant. Far away.

"Oh," he said, his blank tone properly encompassing the hollowness I felt over the matter. "Well," he said, clearing his throat, "you will be high king. No one would blame you if you made an exception. It's one thing to take a bride you don't love, but it's another when there is someone else that you do."

Did I? Did I love someone else? The truth of it was impossible to deny, even in the privacy of my own mind. But it didn't matter. I had a duty. A duty I was born into and I could not abandon now, no matter how unpleasant it was. Mating with Darla would be hard, but I would have to accept the terms. I hadn't made the journey over thousands of miles to quit now.

"I can't. I will not hold you and the others to a standard without following it myself. I cannot be the exception. I must be the example, no matter how wrong it feels. If I'm to rule, I must be able to place my people before myself." I didn't even realize I had been shaking the entire time I was speaking to my brother.

He grimaced. "No one expects you to martyr yourself." He seemed embarrassed for me but empathetic.

I shook my head, resignation settling in. "I'll do what I must. We all will. Now, I should speak to Coel about arranging the ceremony." The words were like bile spilling from my throat.

CHAPTER 16

AMY

"He's mine! *Miiiiine!*" Darla cackled into the phone. Her voice was twisted with malice and smug, arrogant glee.

I looked down, half expecting my stomach to have dropped out of my body. Could she really be engaged to Gardax? It sent my world into a spin. How could he want her? *Her?* I didn't want to see him with anyone, but Darla? That was somehow in a separate universe of awful. He hadn't even tried out the scanner on me. Did it really react to her? How could this be happening?

"You tried to interfere, but nothing was going to stop me from getting what I deserve, what I want. I'm going to be his queen, and you and the rest of this stinking cesspool are going to be nothing more than a distant memory soon." The threatening tone in her voice made my blood run cold, but another thought popped into my head. If Darla was getting what she wanted in the end, didn't that mean that I deserved what I was also promised?

I seized on her words. "So you'll give me Corinne back?" If there was any silver lining to this situation, it was that I'd have my sister back with me and we could start over. I didn't care what happened with Darla and Gardax. They could have each other. I just wanted Corinne, alive and in my arms. I would never let her go after this was over.

I could practically hear her roll her eyes over the phone. "You're such a needy little bitch, you know that?" she spat impatiently.

I didn't answer, just waited. She'd gotten what she wanted, and even if it killed me, I was going to have to make peace with that. But if she didn't deliver my sister back to me safely, she was going to find out who she was really dealing with. I would find her, at any cost. She would have to face my wrath if she wanted to cross me any further.

She sighed. "Whatever, you can have the little shit back." She sounded like she couldn't wait to get rid of Corinne, as if she were simply disposing of the trash.

"When?" I persisted. I wasn't going to dare and hang up the phone until I had received a solid answer from Darla.

"You know, you're starting to get on my nerves. Don't make me punish Corinne for your impertinence," she threatened. "Or maybe I should trade her for you. You can work in the kitchens for my husband and me. I think I'd like the sight of you covered in soot from the oven, waiting on me." She snickered again in that same patronizing tone that made my skin itch.

Bile rose in my throat, but before I could protest, she went on. "Then again, a rat like you can't be trusted. Where are you?" She sounded curious and fearful all at once, as if she were expecting me to come out of nowhere and jab a knife into her aorta.

I didn't want to tell her and put myself at risk, but I wasn't going to get Corinne back by playing hardball, so I told her. I opted for honesty here. I didn't want to give Darla any reason to redact her agreement.

"You'll get the brat back after the wedding is over, when I know you can't try and screw things up any further and I've secured what is mine," she said darkly.

"Okay, when will that be?" I asked. I didn't want to wait around forever. I had been under the impression that as soon as Darla got what she wanted, I'd have my sister back. It just seemed as if she were offering an excuse just to prolong the issue and achieve the upper hand. She had already conquered and won, so what good was it to keep my sister around now?

She hung up without specifying when exactly that would be, but I had a feeling the news would spread quickly. Every fertile female on planet Earth was going to feel the loss of Prince Gardax getting taken off the market. Who was I? Just another hopeless, heartbroken member of the masses. Soon, I would become an afterthought, a refugee out there in the world, suffering and broken just like the rest of them. At least I'd have Corinne by my side.

That's obviously the way he saw me. After everything I said in that message, after knowing what kind of person Darla was, he was still willing to take her. He'd said as much, that he would do whatever he needed for his people. Maybe there was honor in that, but I didn't want to bother looking for it. He must really be desperate to take her back to his planet with him. He could have her, for all I cared. I would just have to shove the pain to the back of my mind where all the rest of the angst dwelled.

Air blasted through the nearly empty room of the abandoned warehouse Bodi and I were hiding out in.

He'd checked in with a contact from the network he got jobs in. Apparently, we were both still wanted outcasts, but it felt good to have someone to share that with. I didn't have to stay out here, out on the run and all alone in the cold. We could keep each other company in order to prevent ourselves from going crazy.

I still had the phone in my hand and he looked at me curiously. "Darla?"

I nodded, struggling to keep calm as I explained, "She and Ga—the prince—are getting married." I took a deep breath as I reeled from voicing that horrid statement out loud.

Not knowing my feelings, he nodded. "That's good news for you, right? Maybe ease some of the heat on your back." He gave me an innocently kind smile.

I looked away, busying myself by pulling out two packets of dried miso to reconstitute for us on the makeshift hot plate Bodi had created. For such a young kid, he really was talented—at least, when he managed to not blow up the things he was working on. But genius didn't come without a price, I suppose. He was the first friend I'd made who hadn't sold me out when it served him, so I managed to overlook the occasional smell of burnt hair. He seemed to really know how to make it out in the cruel world all on his own. I was in good hands, being in his company.

"Yeah. Good news," I managed. "After the wedding, I'll get Corinne back." I sighed again. My voice was depressed and shaky. I was exhausted but surviving on the remaining fumes of the adrenaline from the conversation I'd had with Darla.

"What then?" he asked, taking the metal cup of miso from me. He seemed genuinely interested in what would become of me.

"I don't know. I hadn't really thought that far out just yet," I said, letting the familiar salty, earthy flavor of the hot soup soothe me. I let out a sad and pitiful little chuckle as the warmth of the soup filled my throat and hit my belly with a delicious sensation.

"Well, the posse burned me, so I'm not sticking around here much longer. Think I'll head someplace warmer. Tired of these bitch ass cold winters," he said, a far off, dreamy look in his eyes. I privately wondered what kind of expectations he still clung to and whether he still had any kind of optimism for dreaming of his future.

"Hey, now, language," I warned, as if it'd been Corinne. I guess that was still a of habit, trying to protect her even though she wasn't even here with me.

"Okay, *Mom.*" He rolled his eyes. For a brief moment, I could feel the fragile vulnerability beneath his words. It was awkward but also endearing, and I wished I had a way of helping him out. Unfortunately, I couldn't even manage to take care of myself and Corinne. I didn't have the energy or the resources to add on a third.

"There's lots of warm places. Any particular one in mind?" I asked, changing the subject. I was curious about where he dreamed of. Probably some island that was surrounded with deep blue oceans and white sandy beaches. Somewhere palm trees stretched to the sky and seagulls cawed faintly in the distance.

He nodded. "I grew up in San Clemente. Maybe I'll head back there," he mentioned casually with a shrug, still staring off into space.

"Do you have family there?" I asked. I took a sip of my soup and made a slurping noise as I relished in its flavor. Anything other than tofu tasted delicious and was somewhat of a delicacy to me, even if it was just scraps.

He shook his head and looked down, so I didn't press it. We all had our walls, our emotional No-Man's-

Land. I wasn't going to impose myself on his situation. It was none of my business, and I understood how to stay within the safety net of boundaries.

"I figure it's far enough away from the people after me to get a fresh start." He finally met my gaze and there was a playful twinkle in his eye that disappeared as quickly as it had arrived.

I nodded and thought about that. Escaping the world and running from my problems sounded like a wonderful option, but I'd have to wait until I got Corinne back first if I were ever to flee. It's not like either of us had anything to lose by starting over.

When I got Corinne back, would we stay here? Could I? I didn't think so. I needed a change, needed to forget everything that we'd gone through. I was afraid that everywhere I went, I would be reminded of Gardax, and that wasn't something I was willing to face yet.

"You're welcome to join me, you know, if you have people on you still," Bodi said, not making eye contact. His voice was hushed, as if he were paranoid that someone might pop out of the shadows, listening intently to our conversation.

I looked over at him, smiling to myself. I remembered what it was like to be that age, to have nothing and nobody, to feel lost in the world with people out to get you. It was a good and bad thing. He didn't have any responsibilities like I did, but he was too young to be on his own.

"Maybe. I have to get Corinne back first," I said, wondering what my sister would make of him. He didn't have to help me out and keep my secret or let me share his hideout, and he'd seemed genuinely concerned when he saw what had been happening to Corinne.

"Yeah, yeah, no worries," he quickly answered as if it wasn't something I had to respond to today. I gave him a sideways smile, even though he didn't notice. It was good to have somebody to talk to for once. He was distracting me, in a positive way. He was helping me to see that there were options.

Humanity really was a spectrum. You had the scum of the earth like Darla who thought nothing of torturing innocent children, and then you had people like Bodi, who had nothing but still found compassion, despite whatever trauma he'd endured. I admired the innocent, reflective way he was able to view the world. It was something that I would definitely have to work on. I'd worn my protective shield for a long time now, and suffering had naturally hardened me.

And it pissed me off that someone like Darla got a

happy ending while the ones who tried to do good ended up in a dirty, freezing warehouse. If I dwelled on how unfair life was, though, I would just drive myself crazy. It wasn't worth the mental pain. *Darla* wasn't worth taking up residence in my thoughts.

I opened my bag and pulled out the small, rough blanket I'd grabbed out of my apartment. It was getting dark out, and after the news of Gardax's impending nuptials to that two-faced gorgon, I just wanted to sleep my feelings off. Maybe I would feel better in the morning.

I curled up in a corner of the empty room, closing my eyes and trying not to picture their wedding . . . and their wedding night. Objectively speaking, Darla wasn't the worst-looking woman in the world. I could give her that. It was just her awful personality, her total lack of a soul that took her from decent to horrid.

How could Gardax not see that? I didn't understand how he missed it, or if not that, how he could over-look it. How could he not even try to protest the wedding? Was I missing something here? I'd spent enough time around him by now to know that he was not a superficial person.

I guess it wasn't my place to question it. It was none of my business now. As soon as I got my sister back, we would do our best to press forward, like we always had.

I thought, after he'd gone through the trouble of reassigning me, then tracking me down and chasing me . . . well, it was just damned confusing. My own reaction to *him* didn't help. If he wanted me, he could come and find me. I wasn't going to meddle in dealings that I had no place being a part of.

As I lay there, a montage of all the little daydreams I'd created of the two of us played through my mind. I wrapped myself in the warmth of those false memories. But it wasn't real, and it never would be, because he'd found his match. And if Darla was his perfect match, maybe I was dodging a bullet after all.

Too bad it didn't feel like that. Too bad it felt like my heart was getting ripped out of my body and used as a trampoline. I knew I'd have to endure a fitful sleep and an anxious belly churning inside me.

But loss was familiar enough. I'd learn to forget eventually, I hoped. Gardax would marry Darla and the two of them would go back to his planet, some distant alien paradise.

I wondered absentmindedly about her husband, but if she could do what she did to Corinne and me, I had no doubt that she'd make quick work of disposing of her husband. Hopefully for him, that was a divorce and not something more violent. Of course, with her, who knew?

Either way, this was my new reality, and much as it hurt, I couldn't let this grief destroy me. I would have to move on, no matter the circumstances. I would have to keep my head held high and persevere.

My thoughts became shapeless and blurred when I was suddenly jarred awake. I'd heard a noise that had startled me awake.

Bodi was in the opposite corner, tinkering with something, when a loud metal knocking sound came from the door. We'd piled some debris in front of it for safety while we slept. I motioned to him to stay where he was and he didn't fight me on it.

I wasn't exactly a ninja, but I reached into my pocket, finding my trusty blade and creeping toward the doorway. I had to put on my suit of bravery. It would be my responsibility to protect both of us.

"Ms. Allen?" A male voice said, muffled through the door. I didn't recognize the tone.

I didn't answer as my mind raced over who it could be. Bodi did say that the people Gardax had reached out to were powerful, but why would they still be looking for me now? He'd already been matched with Darla. That should have been the end of the story.

"Ms. Allen, you don't know me, but I know Darla and I know what she's done. I'm here to help." The voice sounded genuine, but I was still scared. I was still distrusting.

My heart caught in my throat. Could I trust that? If they knew Darla, they could be working for her. Engaged to the prince, she had all kinds of money at her disposal now, no doubt. Maybe she'd decided to be vindictive and sent someone to kidnap me. Frankly, with Darla, I had no idea what to expect anymore. No low seemed too low for her. I couldn't allow myself to fall into another one of her plots, schemes, or traps.

"Please, I've done something awful and I'm trying to fix it," the voice called. Something about his tone hit a nerve. I knew guilt well enough, and there was plenty of that laced in with his plea.

Nervously, I moved the metal shelves and other items blocking the door, making a horrible ear-splitting screech as the metal dragged across the concrete floor. I glanced back at Bodi. He was frozen in fear, still cowering on the dirty, dusty floor.

Holding my breath and my knife with equal care, I

opened the door with a white-knuckle grip to be certain that it wouldn't wobble out of my shaking hands.

The man on the other side looked vaguely familiar, but I couldn't place him. He seemed to be in his early forties with an average build and agitated hazel eyes. He sighed when he saw my face, relief washing over his features.

"Thank God. my name is Inez and I need your help."

CHAPTER 17
GARDAX

"Your bride." Darbnix paused, seeming to struggle for the right words. "She's certainly strong-minded." He gave me a sympathetic glance that was so brief it was hard to tell whether I'd even just imagined it.

It was his polite way of correctly saying she was wretchedly demanding and entitled. It had been less than twenty-four hours since I had scanned her and yet she had made it feel like an unending eternity, with her constant complaints and attempts to bully and boss my staff, my brothers, and even, at times, myself.

We hadn't even said our vows yet, and she was already trying to control nearly every aspect of my life. I was embarrassed and had no excuse to give my brothers for her behavior. I was just as befuddled as they were over the whole ordeal.

"Yes," I agreed, letting my voice trail off rather than give voice to the bitterness and doubt that plagued me. Then, dejectedly, I added, "Let us hope you are not so lucky in your chosen mate."

"Indeed," he concurred. "How soon will you return to Erebis then?" I was relieved at his segway into somewhat of a new conversation topic.

Before I could answer, Darla came sweeping into my private chambers unannounced. "There you are," she said, rudely ignoring Darbnix and walking straight toward me with a clack of her heels on the floor.

"I'm making some changes for the party tonight and I need access to your accounts," she said, crossing her arms defiantly as if this request wasn't going to be up for debate.

She was fully attired in the very finest Earth-wear, and yet something about her carriage still seemed gaudy and contrived. My personal secretary had offered her a selection of Trilyn fashions, traditional garb for a royal, but she had declared the items matronly and unsuited to her position.

How she could presume to have any understanding of her role baffled me, but it was hardly the most concerning interaction I had witnessed. I tried to bite my tongue and not start an unnecessary argument, but I was afraid that if she protested the garb I requested her to wear, what else would she refuse?

"What are you talking about? You already have your Earth fund with more than enough for your entertainment and personal care," I said. Finances weren't a concern, but I didn't view her careless greed in a particularly good light. I stared at her, eager to stand my ground on this one.

Darbnix cleared his throat. "Excuse me for interrupting, but what sort of changes did you make? The format and preparations for the party have been carefully planned well in advance."

Darla turned to him with a flash of anger and sneered down her nose. "I believe I was speaking to my future husband," she spat as if Darbnix were an annoying insect she wanted to defensively wave off.

The Neroil kitten in his lap hissed at her, its eyes turning vibrant green and the air around it crackling as it pulsed electromagnetic energy. Another of my brother's menagerie of curiosities and pets. He always carried one with him. It was almost like his trademark. He didn't need security officers surrounding him. He had enough pets to do that work for him.

Darla drew back in a rare expression of fear. "What is that?" she shrieked in horror as if she were bracing herself for an attack.

Darbnix chuckled. "It's okay, Shashti," he said, stroking the kitten's fur with adoration. "She's just a kit. At this age, she's harmless, but in another year, she'll have quadrupled in size and be capable of ripping a man in two with one bite. Fortunately, they're as loyal as they are fierce," he told Darla as the kitten purred and angled its head to allow Darbnix to scratch along its jaw and chin. I gave him an indulged half smile. He was slighting Darla in the process without her observing the same.

Darla stepped closer, warily inspecting the animal. The belled sleeve of her dress dangled with fringe in front of the kitten's face and it batted at the tassels with exposed claws, snagging and tearing the delicate material.

"Hey!" Darla screeched and slapped at the kitten, barely missing it as Darbnix turned and Darla contacted his arm instead.

"Get that monstrous little beast out of here! I don't want some bloodthirsty varmint running loose in here!" Darla recoiled as she stared at Darbnix, simply repulsed.

Shashti bared her teeth again despite Darbnix's murmurs and attempts to sedate the animal. He soothingly stroked its back and whispered pacifying statements into its ears but its green eyes sparked with mutual fury for Darla.

"I'm afraid you're not making a good impression. The Neroil are very sensitive to chakras and energy flows," Darbnix warned and stood to leave. He reached the doorway, and as the passage materialized, he turned back to add, "It is interesting that you see her as a monster. I often find that what we see in the natural world is more a reflection of ourselves than anything else." His lips curled with smug glee.

"Unbelievable! Are you just going to stand there while that brute lets his beasts run wild in here and assault your bride?" She whirled to face me, arms flailing with anger in the air. Her cheeks were flushed in an unflattering crimson color and a few strands of her hair were askew and popping out of the bun she'd curled it in.

"That 'brute' is a prince of the Trilyn and my brother. Furthermore, it was perfectly sedate before your arrival. Now, what do you need more money for?" I raised my tone of voice to curtly imply that neither I, nor anyone in my immediate family, would be addressed in such a disrespectful manner.

"Well, I fired the musicians you had hired. Now, I need money to hire more. I want our wedding to be perfect, after all," she said, her sharpness disappearing beneath a mask of cool control. Her new tone was that of a sullen child whining after realizing they weren't going to easily get their way.

"What was wrong with the musicians we had selected?" I narrowed my eyes and took a step closer to her.

She stepped forward then, a look of sensual aggression on her face as she dragged her fingernails across my chest. The act made me want to leap back but I steeled myself against the urge. I needed to grow accustomed to her proximity. We would be husband and wife in a few short hours, after all. Even if I cringed at the very sight of her, let alone her sadistic touch, I couldn't allow my emotions to crack.

"They were low-class and I don't want some bottom-feeder trash at my wedding," she cooed despite the cold inhumanity of her words. "It's already done anyway. I fired them an hour ago. But now that awful secretary of yours says I can't access any more funds without your agreement." She rolled her eyes as if it shouldn't even be a question that she should be granted complete clearance to my money.

"Well, then, I'll have to disappoint you, because I don't agree," I said with a formal shake of my head.

Her hand lowered and she rubbed along my inner thigh. "Well, what can I do to earn your agreement? I'm a good sport, you know." She batted her eyelashes and gave me a sultry stare.

I stepped back just as she lowered to her knees, unable to bear the contact or the suggestion any longer. "That will not be necessary," I responded indignantly.

Her eyes sparked with icy displeasure. "What? Do you like your whores dirty, is that it? Too bad. You're going to be *mine* soon, you know. This *will* happen, whether you like it or not," she warned darkly as she stood back on her feet. "Don't forget, Gardax, *you* need *me*, and if you want me to play game, I might need some convincing."

Her lips pursed wickedly. Her eyes burned with malice as if she were ready to spit fire directly in my eyes if I didn't play by her rules.

I didn't oblige her with a response. I squared my jaw and took a deep breath, turning to look out the window. I didn't want to face her anymore. I was afraid of what I might say if I looked at her for even one more second. After realizing she wasn't going to receive the satisfaction of me tucking my tail between my legs and agreeing to anything she asked, she stomped out of the room and left me alone with the growing dread I felt over my situation.

Nothing in me stirred for Darla. If anything, it inspired revulsion. She treated everyone as her inferior, she completely lacked humility, and she gave no thought to the feelings of others. None of these attributes boded well for her performance as a Trilyn queen. My queen would need to harbor philanthropy and compassion, charitable characteristics, and a maternal charisma. Something that I knew Darla had none of.

What sort of ruler would she be? Worse, what sort of mother? Her behavior was beginning to reveal a rather cruel, malicious streak that alarmed me greatly. Part of me would rather bear no children than to bring some into the world that might house her same personality characteristics.

As grotesque as the thought of bedding her was, I was even more disturbed at the idea of her having power and influence over any offspring we might create. Would I even be able to perform under the pressure of being in bed with her? Would I even become aroused enough to plant my Trilyn seed into her?

I sat back in a large chair, pouring a hefty glass of Trilynian spirits as I wondered how I would ever manage to go through with the ceremony today. I took a deep breath and rubbed my throbbing temples. I needed to brainstorm a way out of this arranged marriage, but my mind was too shocked and exhausted to come up with anything reasonable.

At Darla's insistence, we were set to wed before the party tonight, which would then double as a reception. She was pressing the issue and breathing down my neck, barking orders to everyone who was unfortunate enough to cross paths with her. It was as if she were desperate to get on with the ceremony so that she would officially be my bride.

It all felt so wrong. This wasn't how it was supposed to go. How could Darla possibly be the right woman for me? That was a dangerous thought, and it led me to think again of the woman that everything in me told me *was* the right one. My heart still ached for her. I yearned to touch her creamy skin and to feel the tickle of her braid against my cheek.

Where *was* Amy? Her disappearance was still a mystery to me and added to my discontentment over this affair with Darla. The scanners always read true, there was no arguing with science, but I'd never gotten the chance to scan Amy. I still needed closure before I could get on with this vile wedding to Darla.

It was preposterous to consider that I could have two perfect matches, I knew, but the question remained. Until I knew for certain, I wouldn't be able to concentrate on anything else, certainly not the wedding ceremony to a wretched, hostile woman like Darla.

I set my drink down, deciding to summon Coel to rush the search for Amy, by any means necessary. Surely, there must be someone we could bribe, *something* that we could do. I just knew that if I didn't see her again, if I didn't have the chance to scan her, the uncertainty would plague me forever. She seemed scared to face me on her own, for fear of her sister's safety.

As I went to put the glass down, I saw my phone. When I grabbed it, the screen lit, declaring a message —the message I had forgotten to check in the resulting chaos of Darla's scanner reading. Everything had been a murky blur ever since then.

I selected it and lifted the speaker to my ear. My heart drummed anxiously in my chest. I could barely breathe with the anticipation of what I might hear.

"Gardax, it's Amy. Please, I need your help. I'm sorry I ran from you. I'm sorry I couldn't tell you what's going on, but she was watching me, tracking me, and she would have hurt my sister if she knew I reached out to you.

She? I struggled to untangle her message as my pulse leaped. Amy's voice sounded crackly and frightened. My mind swirled in an abyss of confusion.

"It's Darla. My supervisor. When I first started working for you, she acted like a friend, but the more I got to know her, the more I saw the cracks in her veneer. She turned around and used every weakness she found in me to bully and control me. I could have handled all that, but then she took my sister.

If I had reached out to you, told you what was going on, she said she'd hurt Corinne. I'm sending this message to you as a last resort. Everything is spiraling way out of control. Please, I've got nowhere else to turn. call me when you get this."

The message ended with her pleading tone shaking me to the core. It took several moments for my fists to relax from the white-knuckled balls they'd curled into. Amy's voice reached directly to the most sensitive part of me. She was afraid, and my immediate reaction was to eliminate whatever threat had put her into such a position.

So Darla was behind Amy's disappearance? What kind of person does such a thing as taking a child hostage for blackmail? And why would she have tried to cut Amy off from me? She hadn't done the same to any of the other kitchen workers I'd interviewed. It didn't make sense. Fury consumed me. I didn't' even realize the height of my anger until my jaw began to ache because I'd clenched it so tight.

Every instinct in me wanted to react, to protect Amy. But, I knew that to do so would mean that I would be failing my people. How could it have come to this? I paced the floor, trying to make sense of something that was so diluted with emotional clutter that I didn't know if I'd ever reach a solution.

In my heart, I knew I could never align myself with someone capable of such cruelty, such depravity. If it were true, I could not marry her. But with so much at risk, could I afford to believe this without evidence? There had to be some way to discover the source, but how? There were a million questions trolling my brain, and they were urgent, with no sign of getting any closer to finding Amy.

Every personal inclination led me to believe Amy's accusations against Darla, but there was another layer to consider. If Darla really held Amy's sister, if Corinne really was in danger, I needed to be sure that Darla acted alone. If I acted too quickly, if I alerted Darla to my knowledge of her actions, I risked further harm to Amy's sister. Did I have any choice but to play along with this wretched game? I certainly didn't want to be the reason something terrible happened to Amy's sister. I would have to play my cards right and cautiously weigh the options.

There were too many questions left unanswered, and my duty warred with emotions greater than I'd ever known. I felt a pull toward Amy, but on the other hand, I knew the scanner didn't lie. Deep down, there had to be a way to follow my heart while ensuring the future of my people at the same time.

CHAPTER 18

AMY

"What do you want?" I asked, unsure why someone would be coming to me for help when I couldn't manage to help myself. I gave the strange man a scowl and took an instinctive and reluctant step backward.

"May I please come in?" the man asked, craning his neck to curiously search behind me.

I was unsure, but at this point, what did I have to lose? With the exception of Darla, I was generally a decent judge of character, or at the very least, who was a threat and who wasn't. I'd been right about her. It was hard for me to read this man's neutral demeanor so far.

Apprehensive, I stepped aside, allowing him to enter the room. He looked around and caught sight of Bodi.

"Who is this?" he asked, more curious than demanding.

Bodi, still holding the device he'd been tinkering with, stood and puffed his chest. "Who wants to know?" he asked, the screwdriver tight in his hand. My lips curled with amusement. The kid could stand up for himself after all.

I hadn't known him long enough to know his tells, but the screws he'd loosened on the machine he held rattled just faintly and I felt a surge of protectiveness. I was warming up to him. I wished I could help him and not bury him in the mess of my own problems.

I stepped between them, raising my knife once more as a threat. "You came here for help, then tell me what it is you need and quickly. I won't ask again." My eyes seared into the strange man. I wasn't playing games.

He looked faintly alarmed for a moment and raised his hands in a gesture of surrender. "Okay, okay, I'm not here to harm you." He flicked his glance nervously between me and Bodi.

He looked forlorn, sad, pacing the floor. Something troubled him, and I wasn't sure I wanted to be dragged into it, but if he knew my name and how to find me, then it seemed I had little choice in the matter.

When he didn't speak right away, I cleared my throat, giving him a gentle coaxing, but it would be the last time I indulged him with something other than a knife to his throat if he didn't get to spilling his conscience soon.

Inez glanced my way. "First, let me apologize. I never meant . . . I did not realize you or your sister would be harmed." He trailed off in a regretful tone.

He glanced furtively at me, and my ears pricked and my heart raced, waiting for him to continue. He was being too vague. He needed to hurry up and hash out whatever it was that he came here to confess.

"When I came with Prince Gardax to Earth, it was a second chance for me. The virus on our planet, it was violent and swift, sweeping through whole cities in a night, before anyone even knew it had reached them. It started in the heart of Trilynia—Erebis—carried there, we believe, by some space refuse or aboard one of the ships that regularly dock there for intergalactic trade. The source matters little, though."

He paused, taking a deep breath as if steadying himself before he would be able to have the mental and physical courage to go on.

"From there, it swept outward, reaching every continent in a matter of weeks, despite our best efforts to contain it. It mutated constantly, with the method of transmission changing slightly with every incarnation, making it difficult to defend against and impossible to predict. For those with weak immunities, the very old, the very young, and those . . . those like my wife, who was pregnant with our first child, it sometimes proved lethal."

I watched as he closed his eyes, stemming the emotion that warred to break free. I felt for his loss, could see the struggle he endured to block the pain. His eyes were sad and reclusive for a moment before he finally took a deep breath and continued.

Blinking rapidly, he sighed and went on. "But for most, its effects were not so severe. Dizziness, headache, loss of energy, mild neuropathy, slight muscle atrophy in some. Initially, it was treated as more of a nuisance by our authorities. That is, until its full effects became clear. The Trilyn race was almost entirely rendered infertile before anyone noticed." He took a breath to glance up at me and

Bodi, gauging our reactions. I still didn't know what this had to do with my sister and how he could help me, but I exhibited as much patience as I could.

"When I came here to assist the princes, it was to get away from what I had lost. Distance didn't solve everything, however, and I did anything I could to insulate myself from the pain. I'm not proud to admit that included developing a friendship with Darla."

"You're *friends?*" I asked, incredulous. How could anyone be friends with that wretch? I wondered before recalling I had once fallen for her act. She was a snake in the grass, a wolf in sheep's clothing. Manipulation was her trade.

He cringed. "So to speak. She offered me *comfort* of a kind." When I didn't comprehend his initial meaning, he clarified, "We began a physical relationship. One which I now regret, because it came at a cost. At first, the promise was that I would take her with me when I returned, but eventually, that stopped being enough." He sagged his shoulders and hung his head in regretful disgrace.

"She manipulated me into assisting her and I . . . I shamed myself by going along, too afraid of the consequences of turning back, of losing the only thing I had left, my work. You see, I developed the gene sequencing technology that identifies and computes compatibility for the scanners that the princes have used."

What was I hearing? What was he saying? I knew, and I didn't know. My mind reeled while my body stood in perfect stillness. It was like putting together two puzzle pieces that you couldn't see. You could only feel how well they fit, how snugly they fell into place, though you didn't know why just yet. There was understanding and confusion swirling through my head. Was this guy the genius behind the scanners? Did he really help Darla in manipulating their functions?

"When Darla learned that the prince had found a match in the kitchens, she forced me to create a scrambler. It's a device that interferes with the scanner's system to result in a false positive reading." He gulped and grimaced as if he were afraid to meet my gaze, but he bravely did so anyway.

The wind seemed to rush out of my lungs. "What are you saying? Are you telling me . . . Darla . . . she's not . . ." it was too much, the well of hope that rose in me. "Darla isn't Gardax's mate?" My voice was shrill with hopeful excitement.

"No." He shook his head. "But he wouldn't have realized that for a while. The scanners were created because while humans are immune to the virus that attacked the Trilyn, and though we are genetically similar enough to allow reproduction, there is enough variation to make it difficult, if not impossible, to conceive without optimal compatibility."

My mind raced with possibility and apprehension. Did I dare to hope? Who would be left besides me to scan from the kitchens that night?

"Why now? Why have you changed your mind and why do you need *my* help?" I asked. I took a step forward, but I didn't mean to lunge at him. He cowered defensively and shielded himself with his arms.

"Because I reminded him of his duties to our people," a deep voice boomed from the doorway.

We all turned to see someone new, a tall man with smooth dark skin and pale eyes the color of seafoam, so piercing that I knew in an instant he must be related to Gardax. I held my breath and paused, waiting to see what this man would do upon entering the room.

"And who's this guy?" Bodi asked, gaining some confidence despite the very muscular new presence. He stood proudly next to me as if he were just waiting for a brawl to ensue so that he could have the opportunity to use the screwdriver in his fist.

The newcomer had to duck to make it through the doorway. "I am Prince Darbnix of Noor, Gardax's brother. I sensed that something was not right with Gardax's match and I went in search of answers. And you" —he looked to me— "are the only hope we have of stopping the mess this traitor has made." His lips curled into a stoic smile as if he were coming with the intention of making a truce before we'd even formally met.

I looked back to Inez, who nodded and looked downcast. "The prince is right. I used to be a good man, someone who acted with honor. I lost sight of that and I became this, a cowardly shell of my former self. Anything good in me died with my wife. Without her, I am broken. I had neither the courage nor the conviction to face what I had done until the prince confronted me." He gestured awkwardly at Darbnix standing behind him.

Darbnix surveyed me thoughtfully and spoke with the measured calm of someone used to being listened to. "Ms. Allen, it is a great deal to ask for your assistance when you have been so harmed simply by your proximity to my family, but I have tried to reason with my brother and he has numbed himself to his sacrifice. He goes forward with this only because he believes he is ensuring the survival of our people, and yet he still searches for you. I cannot stir in him the emotions I have seen when you were mentioned, and I fear it is the only way to reach him now."

My stomach fluttered at Darbnix's explanation even as I marveled at the tiny face that appeared in his pocket. A fluorescent pink reptilian face blinked at me as beseechingly as Prince Darbnix. I felt honored that he cared enough to seek me out and help me in this time of uncertainty.

They all looked to me with hope, waiting for me to agree to assist them, but could I? I wasn't so sure. I shifted my weight uncomfortably. I was in the hot seat.

"I'm not sure I can. I sent a message already to Gardax, laying out what Darla had done to me, and he's apparently prepared to overlook that."

Darbnix spoke first. "Gardax is in misery, of that I am certain. I cannot read my brother's mind to tell you what he knows or does not, but I know behavior and I can tell you he is tormented. Every time he looks at

Darla, I see him flinch and recoil, even if it's only slightly. He's too proud to admit that something might be amiss with the scanners."

I chewed on my lip as I debated. Could I open myself up to that again? To the possibility, only to be crushed and left broken again? What if I wasn't the real match either? I didn't know how I could recover from that emotional trauma.

"Trilynia will not be the only one to suffer if Gardax marries Darla. Her lust for power is boundless and she will tolerate no threats to that. I have every reason to believe that once she has gotten what she wants, she will kill your sister, and possibly, you as well . . . perhaps even me," Inez said. His voice sounded desperate and weak.

"Damn, that's some heavy stuff." Bodi sighed from across the room. I glanced back at him and he was nodding as if he were proud to be engaged in the conversation with the rest of us.

Inez looked to me, sorrow and regret etched in his features. "Will you help us?" I could feel the weight of the world in his stare, as if I were his only chance at redeeming his past mistakes.

I sighed, closed my eyes, and despite the uncertainty and fear at war within me, I answered, "I will." I didn't even recognize my voice as I impulsively belted out the assertion. "I will help," I proclaimed a second time to make it more believable in my mind.

Darbnix came forward then, and I saw the pack at his back. "Good, then we have no time to lose. The wedding proceedings will be underway shortly." He was formal and serious. His features were plagued with the gravity of the situation.

"Today?" I asked in shock. "He is marrying her today?" I couldn't believe it. The wind was suddenly knocked out of me again and I had a sour taste in my mouth. My stomach churned with acid and sickness.

Darbnix nodded, lowering the pack and opening it. "Darla demanded it and Gardax is too heartbroken to see what's really going on."

I nodded, hurt for Gardax, hurt for myself, hurt even for Inez. There were a ton of kinks to iron out, but would we be able to make it in time?

"What is this?" I asked, confused as Darbnix began to pull out brightly colored fabrics. I took a step forward to be able to better inspect the garments with simple curiosity.

"Darla has put restrictions on who can and can't come to the party, the first flex of her control, no doubt," Darbnix answered. "You will have to accompany me as a guest. It's the only way to ensure you will be allowed on the ship without question. And looking as you do, lovely though you are, I fear you will be recognized and Darla alerted. This," he said, unfolding a gorgeously shimmering gown, "is your disguise." He gave me a sentimental smile. I could see the kindness and warmth in his eyes, just like I felt with Gardax. These were good men, and they deserved better than what they were getting.

A tremulous smile crossed my lips as I reached out and touched the buttery soft fabric. It was white, and it wasn't. When it moved, it caught the light and shimmered, fracturing into a rainbow of colors that danced like light on water. It was simply stunning, and I couldn't believe I would have the luxury of being able to wear it.

"It's beautiful," I breathed, captivated by how ravishing it was.

"It's Trilynian." Darbnix smiled as if he were humbled and appreciated the compliment of my reaction. "Now let's go," he urged, pulling out a pair of intricately beaded slippers and pins.

I grabbed the dress, and the men left the room, giving me privacy. I placed the dress over my head and spun around, even though I didn't have a mirror.

I breathed a sigh. This was a blissful dream to be draped in such fine attire.

Hurriedly, I discarded my clothes, long tunic, thin leggings, ratty socks and boots, and a well-worn jacket, the unofficial uniform of a refugee. I tried to remember the last time I'd even worn clothes that weren't dirty and tattered.

The room was growing colder by the minute as the sun receded from the sky, and the chill and the other-worldly dress made my body seem almost foreign to me. I looked down at myself swathed in finery and couldn't help but wonder if I wouldn't wake up soon to find myself still napping in that corner. Had I blurred the lines of fantasy and reality once again? But here I was. This wasn't a dream.

I unmade my thick braid and piled the curling waves into a mass at my crown, putting the pins Darbnix had given me into place to secure the impromptu style. For one of the first times ever, I regretted that I had no makeup, but when I caught my reflection in a piece of broken glass, I didn't dislike what I saw. The adornments Darbnix gave me were lovely, but I could still see myself beneath them. I didn't find myself worthy of wearing such delicacy.

As I walked quickly to the door to join them, I grabbed

one last thing. Reaching into my jacket, I pulled out my switchblade. I may be dressed like one of those gilded upper-caste women, but I would fight for myself and the people I love like the refugee I'd always been.

"Whoa." Bodi laughed. "You about to shut that party down. No way the prince marries Darla after he sees you." He laughed lightheartedly.

Darbnix smiled appraisingly. "Everything is more convincing from the lips of a beautiful woman." His eyes twinkled as he gave me a respectable wink.

I blushed. "Well, let's just hurry." I wasn't used to receiving this amount of favorable attention, but we didn't have time to sit here and dish about how stunning I looked or didn't look. The clock was ticking, and Darla was still out there.

Darbnix led me to a transport shuttle outside the warehouse where Bodi and I had been encamped. At my insistence, Inez agreed to bring Bodi aboard the ship under the guise of an apprentice. I'd made it this far because of him, and I wasn't about to leave him behind now.

The shuttle ride was quick, and when we disembarked, it was in a different dock than the staff entrance. There were a number of shuttles arriving, carrying guests for the party. My heart raced in anticipation and I prayed that I wouldn't be recognized by anyone in attendance.

"Darla insisted the wedding be a surprise to announce once the festivities of the party began," Darbnix informed me, whispering in my ear as we shuffled through the drones of people.

"Of course, she'd want to gloat, to crow over everyone she feels she's superior to now," I answered darkly and narrowed my eyes.

A guard came to our shuttle, but seeing Prince Darbnix, he bowed and allowed us entrance. It felt surreal walking among all the dainty, delicate guests. I was out of place and out of my element, but I had Darbnix by my side to subtly coach me along.

But we didn't have time for me to feel out of place. Once we'd moved into the main hail, Darbnix pulled me with him down a side passage. He yanked me with a frantic desperation that alarmed my senses.

Winding through a series of doors that appeared out of nowhere, passages filled with servants, and beautifully anointed rooms, we finally made it. My heart was in my throat, but I was still breathing.

Darbnix stopped and whispered hurriedly to the guard as Bodi and Inez caught up to us. In a matter of seconds, the wall vanished, and it felt like almost as if we had fallen out of the ship. I tried to stifle a scream by clamping my hand over my mouth. I hadn't been expecting that to happen.

The floor, the ceiling, the walls, all of it was transparent but for a faint, rippling shimmer. It was like we floated, suspended by some unknown force, in the vast emptiness of space. Strange floating candles like tiny, brilliant stars hung in the air. It was an out of body experience. I twisted the skin of my wrist to make sure I wasn't dreaming.

"Prince Gardax, Ruler of Erebis, heir to High Throne of Trilynia, do you pledge your troth, by the sacred seal of the Trilyn, to take this woman to wife?" A woman with caramel skin and knee-length black locks stood at the far end of the room where Gardax stood with Darla, their backs to us.

My heart pounded in my chest, and without thinking it through, I simply called out to him, "Gardax!" It was urgent, impulsive. I spoke before my mind had a chance to convince me not to.

Shocked, he turned toward me. His eyes scanned me as if I might not be real and then finally locked with mine. He stared at me, completely bewildered.

Darla glared with devilish ferocity at me but grabbed

Gardax's arm, demanding he complete the ceremony. "Answer her!" she screeched.

I stood frozen as I heard the words fall from his mouth, my chest squeezing at the sound. He was robotic, as if he weren't really emotionally in the same zone as his body.

"No," Gardax answered after a long pause.

Silence preceded the wretched sound of Darla's screeching. "*Whaaaaaat?!*"

"No," he repeated, pronouncing the word more clearly. He began to shake his head as the phantom of his tormented state of mind began to lift like a fog.

Darla whirled around. "*You!* You filthy little low-class whore! You are not ruining this for me!" Spittle dribbled down her chin. Hysteria burned in her eyes and her chest heaved with deep, sharp, ragged breaths.

She charged, sprinting with a speed I would not have thought her capable in her gaudy four-inch clear heels. I was her intended target.

Reacting with the 'low-class' instincts I'd earned through years of survival, I turned, sidestepping the strike she meant to land on my face, and reaching into my up-do, I pulled out my switchblade, holding it to her side as she froze in place with the realization that she'd lost.

"You're going to pay for this," she seethed with hatred.

"No. you are," I whispered back with the relief of finally being free to stand up to her. There was no way out. She was trapped.

CHAPTER 19

GARDAX

"**A**rrest her!" Darla demanded, still held in place by Amy's knife at her side.

I was momentarily frozen in shock, mainly from seeing Amy arrive as if to come to my rescue. I stared at her. She had her eyes locked on Darla, knife glistening in the light.

The guards didn't move, looking to me for direction, but I was still too dazed at Amy's presence to speak.

"Arrest this scheming bitch, damn it! I'm your queen!" she cried with bitter petulance. Her voice echoed through the silence.

"Not yet, you're not, and you won't ever be, once everyone hears the truth," Darbnix answered with a harsh tongue.

The rest of my brothers crowded around. "What's going on?" Manzar grumbled. The rest looked perplexed.

"She's not your match," Amy said, looking to me. "She tricked you. She fooled all of you," she said, looking around the room.

"Shut up, you lying wretch!" Darla spat, squirming in Amy's grip.

"You, be quiet," Darbnix warned. "Or I'll bring Shashti out and we'll see what she makes of you now." He glared at Darla as if she were the scum of the planet.

Darla glared but stilled, her eyes darting in an angry panic around her, as if sensing the tide had turned against her fully. She was on the defensive, looking for a way to weasel out of this one.

Amy looked back at me and my heart stilled in my chest at the sincerity and pain in her eyes. "She took my sister and blackmailed me into staying away from you, Gardax, and then she manipulated one of your scientists to create a device that interferes with your scanner, making you believe she was your ideal match, when in reality, she is not. She manipulated me, she abused my sister, and she deceived you. She's not your match."

Before I could answer, Manzar cut in. "And how do we know this is all true?" he demanded, arms crossed. He didn't know anything about Amy, not like I did. His cynical tone cut through the air.

"Because I helped her. My deepest apologies, Your Highnesses. It is with great shame and humiliation that I must own to the truth of these statements. I conspired with this fraud to deceive Prince Gardax into believing she was his mate. But it is not true."

He stepped forward and ripped off what had appeared to be a simple metal bracelet that Darla wore and held it up, revealing a tiny web of circuitry on the inside of the band. "This is the evidence of my disgrace." The man looked pained and shamed all at once, his face displaying grief and remorse.

"No!" Darla screamed, "I'll kill you for this! You son of a bitch! You're nothing more than a backstabbing, sniveling loser! They're lying to you, Gardax. Your brother is trying to take the throne for himself. He's trying to prevent you from having children of your own so that when he kills you, he'll inherit it all! Don't listen to them!" She was shrieking maniacally.

Shouting erupted, sweeping the scene into chaos. Everyone's eyes were wide with confusion and shock. I didn't blame them. This was turning out to be quite a spectacle.

"Enough!" I said loudly. "I've heard enough lies." I walked toward Amy and Darla. "Release her," I demanded.

Amy's eyes went wide but she did as I asked. She had a stung look on her face as if she were wounded by my reaction.

Darla pulled back quickly, springing toward me. "Ha! See! I told you, I would have what is mine." She snickered with a pathetic laugh.

Placing a hand on her shoulder, I turned toward her and looked deeply into her eyes. "Yes, you will have everything that is meant for you. Coel, take this treacherous deviant into custody." Finally, I was able to expel the one statement that I had been longing to say for so long.

"No! Gardax, wait!" she screamed, trying to grab onto me, but Coel was already there, placing her into temporary partial paralysis with a Neural Oscillation Disruptor. Her eyes went wide. Her mouth went slack.

Darla's arms dropped by her side, and while she growled and struggled against the neural interference, she couldn't overcome it enough to form whatever hateful words were on her tongue. She looked as if she were having a convulsion in reaction.

I turned away from her then and went to Amy, taking her hand in mine, hardly believing that she was truly there before me. Her kind eyes warmed my heart and a contented sensation overcame me.

"I don't know how to begin to apologize for everything you've been through, but allow me to start making things right?" I asked, raising her hand to my mouth and pressing a kiss there. Electrical volts of sensual chemistry rippled through my bones.

She trembled at the contact, and I nearly lost myself, but there would be time for that later. If everything worked out, we had a lifetime to explore each other's bodies in the most sensual ways imaginable.

I turned to Darla, anger returning in a mighty storm as I looked upon the vile, greedy creature who would have stolen my future from me. She was flinching and sputtering. Her nose was running and she looked like a maniac being held captive, a rabid animal.

"You stand accused of several serious crimes against the Trilyn Royal Council and your own people. As we are aboard my ship, per the treatise we have struck with the Union, you are under my jurisdiction. Trilyn law establishes that the punishment for such crimes as yours is the brisk death of space release. We are a people of reason and integrity and believe in the swift, impartial administration of justice."

Her eyes went wide with terror at my words as they sank in with harsh reality. She was in terrible trouble, and the color drained from her face.

"However, your crimes are not yet fully settled. You have kidnapped and imprisoned an innocent young girl. If you lead us to her and she is recovered in good health, I may consider your cooperation as a mitigating factor," I explained.

Darla's eyes darted back and forth between myself and Amy, resignation and fear settling there. I nodded to Coel, who reduced the strength of the neural interference.

Darla stretched her jaw, as if getting used to the feel of it once more.

"Well?" I demanded. Was she really debating this? Did she not understand the danger she was in?

She huffed angrily. "Yes, fine, I'll tell you where she is." She flicked her gaze to the floor and fumed in fresh anger. It was either cooperate with us or face imminent death. The choice should be simple.

"Go now. Take a team and follow her directions. Bring the girl back here as soon as you've located her," I directed Coel, who nodded and prodded Darla to walk in front of him.

With them gone, Rawklix whistled. "So, what now? Can we go to the party or what?" Leave it to my youngest brother to want to get down to the real entertainment of the evening.

I shook my head, exasperated with my youngest brother. "Go do what you will. I need to find Lifiya. You," I said to Inez, "You will come with us."

He agreed and the small group of us—Amy, Darbnix, Inez, me, and a young boy who had apparently assisted Amy during this tumultuous ordeal—went to find Lifiya.

Her reaction was what I expected, bewildered and mortified at the misapplication of the technology she had helped to create. After a good deal of convincing, I finally assured her she was not to blame for the situation.

As for Inez, I was sure what to do with him, but now was not the time to deal with him. He kept glancing at me periodically with eyes laced with panic and fear.

The two of them set to clearing and reprogramming my scanner, which had been returned to the lab once Darla had been proven as a match. My heart drummed in my chest. I was anxious to get the device up and running again.

While were waiting, Coel found us. Corinne had not been kept very far. Darla, in her hubris, had hidden her in a storage container in the closet of her private office, aboard my ship, no less.

"Corinne!" Amy cried, seeing her sister.

The girl looked terrible and I felt a fresh assault of guilt upon seeing the damage Darla had heaped upon the poor child, all so she could secure her grasp on me. She was dirty, with sunken bags of exhaustion underneath her skin. She looked as if she'd endured hell and torture. There were marks, scrapes, and bruises all over her body.

Her hair was clipped in shocks of varying lengths, some parts exposing her scalp and revealing painful gashes. One eye was blackened, her bottom lip split, and small, circular burns angrily dotted her exposed arms and neck.

"I didn't know if I'd ever see you again. I'm so sorry!" Amy sobbed, embracing her as gently as she could.

Corinne's eyes squinted, as if adjusting to the light from so many hours in darkness. She looked around, wearily and with a nervous expression of distrust. I couldn't blame the poor girl.

Despite Amy's fawning and emotional reaction, the girl was quiet, almost stoic. I did not have a lot of experience with victims of trauma, but it was clear Darla had left scars more than the ones on her arms, and I hated myself for being complicit, knowingly or not, in the abuse for even a moment.

Now, at least, I would do what I could to ensure her recovery and offer whatever support she needed. I would ensure that she had medical care and attention as we attempted to nurse her back to emotional and physical health.

"I have a team of doctors who can oversee her care, if you will allow," I said gently, placing a hand on Amy's shoulder as she held her sister tightly against her. Amy looked as if she never wanted to let her sister go but was also afraid of damaging her if she squeezed too hard against her sister's frail body.

Breathing in deeply, she pulled back and looked at Corinne. "Are you okay with that?" She tenderly stroked her cheek.

Corinne nodded, just once, but didn't say anything. She mainly kept her eyes planted to the floor.

A blanket was brought out and Amy wrapped Corinne in it, who finally closed her eyes. "Amy?" she squeezed in a pitiful voice that ripped through my heart.

"Yes?" she asked through tears, stroking her

Corinne's face. She was grinning at her sister so fondly as if she were an angel she dreamed of and didn't see in reality.

"I'm okay. Sister's oath," she said, raising her fingers in a little salute. "And you look pretty. I told you you needed a makeover." The girl had a witty quip after all the torture she'd been through. I admired her for that.

Laughing through their tears, they hugged again as I watched, touched by the genuine affection they shared. A chair was wheeled in for Corinne, and after two attendants assured Amy that her sister would be well cared for, she finally allowed her to be taken to the medical chambers.

"Your Highness?" Lifiya came into the room, Inez behind her staring only at his feet while a guard hovered beside him. "We've rebalanced your scanner." She gave me an apologetic smile.

She stretched out her arm as she handed the small device to me, and I took it, suddenly aware of the question that had burned me from the first time I'd laid eyes on Amy but which I was no longer sure I had a right to ask.

I looked to Amy, who was watching me nervously. It was a pivotal moment. I was almost too anxious to point it in her direction. My heart ached for it to light up as soon as it was near her.

"Well?" she asked, staring back at me with those incredible eyes of hers. She was arrestingly beautiful, dressed in the fashions of my people, her hair twisted and secured into a delicate, riotous affair. Everything about her was so pure, so genuine, so perfect. She was the perfect epitome of beauty, captivating and breathtaking in every way.

I set it down and took her hands, oblivious to the people looking on. "I don't need to turn this on. I don't need this machine to tell me what I have suspected from the first moment I saw you or what every moment since has confirmed in my own heart. You are everything that I could have ever dreamed of and so much more. You *are* my perfect match. But what I ask, what I must ask as the future High King of my people, it's too much to ask of anyone. You have already endured so much pain because of me. How could I impose any more?

"I will not turn this on. I will not place that burden upon your shoulders, not unless you want me to. If you wish, I will leave you with enough money that you, Corinne, your children, your children's children will never lack for anything. You can live your lives here, secure, comfortable, cared for, far away from the dangers and stress my position invites, if that is what you want."

Her eyes softened, then lit up, then she frowned. She was concocting a web of emotions in her mind, part of which were revealed in the way she stared at me. "What about your people?" she asked in a gentle whisper.

"I will do what I can for my people. I will sacrifice every bit of myself for them if I need to, but I cannot sacrifice another. I would share my life with you, if you would have it, but the choice is yours. I will not coerce or compel you with the weight of my own obligations."

She looked away then, her hand slipping from mine as her eyes sparkled with moisture. "My whole life, I've struggled. I've struggled to protect my sister, struggled to eat, to find work, to just make it through to another day. But through all of it, I've survived."

My heart clenched with every step she took away from me, but I said nothing, knowing her decision must be hers and hers alone. I didn't even dare to breathe.

Silence settled over the room as she stared off into space. Darbnix stepped forward, looking as though he might try to persuade her, but I held up my hand to silence him. This was not his battle, but I owed him a lot for what he did for me in trying to capture Darla and bring her to justice.

And then she turned around. "I don't want to just survive anymore. I want to *live*," she said, smiling through her tears. "Turn it on." Her voice was strong-willed, defiant, like a martyr.

But before I did, I pulled her into my arms, embracing her finally, content just to stay there, holding her for the rest of our lives. I wanted to freeze this moment in my memory, no matter what happened.

"I love you," I whispered quietly against her ear so that only she could hear. It was our private moment, and it was the truth.

Before she could respond, I switched the device on and the room filled with the glowing pulse of the scanner's light, eclipsed only by the radiance of my own happiness. I gasped, then cried, then laughed with joy, all while holding Amy delicately in my arms. The swell of elation sent me on a euphoric trip and I couldn't believe how lucky I was in that moment. Amy was mine. It was official. The proof was in the glowing illumination of the device.

EPILOGUE
AMY

"Congratulations, Brother," Darbnix said, smiling happily as the scanner in Gardax's hand glowed and trembled with vibrations. I watched it glowing, completely mesmerized and overjoyed to be his match.

"So, is there going to be another alien wedding or what?" Bodi asked awkwardly, earning a chuckle from everyone.

I glanced over at him with a smile. I was over the moon. I held Gardax's hands as he squeezed me tenderly with enough affection to power the whole party.

Gardax looked only at me. "I don't wish to leave another moment up to chance. I would make you mine here and now, but I also want to treat you to whatever your heart desires. If you want a grand, elaborate affair to be broadcast to the whole of the galaxy, then, my lady, that is what you shall have." He gave me a noble bow, and I admired how much of a gentleman he was to me.

I laughed and blushed and blinked back tears all at once. How could this have all happened to me? My heart was exhausted by everything that had happened and my mind was still struggling to come to grips with this new reality. I would be his bride. *Him*, the man I dreamed about constantly. Those daydreams, those fantasies, were all about to become *real*. I was still mentally spinning with glee as I tried to come to terms with my new life. The life I had always dreamed of was now mine to embrace.

And I couldn't wait another minute for that. The glory, the wonderful reality of Gardax as my matched mate, I wouldn't wait another second to make it official.

"We've got our whole lives to throw a party. I'm a simple girl with simple desires, and right now, I just want to be yours." I smiled up at him, my beautiful, incredible alien prince. It was simple. Our love was pure. We didn't need flashy frills to declare our alliance and union with one another.

"Then that is what you shall have." He nodded happily, with a look of some relief, as if he thought I might want to wait another second before my fantasies came to life. My heart was leaping with joy. Everything I ever wanted was finally unfolding before my eyes. It was whimsical and perfect.

The ceremony was short and to the point, exactly as I would have wished it. We repeated the traditional troths and oaths of the Trilyn, pledging our fidelity and love to one another until the end of time and space.

Then, before the handful of Gardax's brothers who could be extracted from the party going on elsewhere on the ship, Corinne, who was dressed in soft, warm Trilyn garments and escorted by one of the royal doctors, Bodi, Lifiya, and Darla, who was once more restrained and prevented from speaking, we kissed and sealed the ceremony, joining our lives and hearts. It was a magical moment that was both private between us and shared among everyone in attendance.

It was tender and gentle. And then it wasn't. With everyone looking on, the kiss slowly grew hungrier, more passionate, until finally, Gardax's youngest brother, Rawklix, coughed loudly, awkwardly breaking us up as we breathed and panted heavily into each other's ears. We were both staring at each other, lust-gazed and lovestruck.

"Looks like someone has been enjoying my Tora Pollen, after all," he joked, laughing playfully.

Pulling back from my lips just enough to speak, Gardax answered succinctly, "Wrong. Neither of us has had a trace." He gazed passionately into my eyes.

Then, scooping me up into the hard strength of his arms, he carried me straight out of the room, earning more than a few whoops of laughter that left me blushing. The wedding ceremony was everything I could have ever imagined, and more.

Later, I knew I'd have to figure out the webbing maze of this place, but as Gardax carried me, my focus was only on him. His smooth olive skin glistened in the starlight that lit the dark passages, and the striking intensity of his yellow eyes never left my face. It was as if he was afraid I'd disappear if he dared look away.

If I'd been capable of speaking, I might have finally gushed about how beautiful he was, how much I'd dreamed of his doing just this, but I was rendered mute by the sheer force of my desire, my passion, my love for him. Nothing mattered right now except for our hungry passion for each other.

I wasn't really aware of what room we were in until

finally, we passed through a set of sheer curtains and I felt him lowering me to an impossibly soft mattress. My body melted into it at once and I let out a contented sigh. I felt weightless, as if I were drifting through the clouds.

I closed my eyes then opened them again quickly. When nothing happened, I pinched my arm and bit down on my lip hard.

Gardax laughed. "What are you doing?"

"I've dreamed about this so many times, of being here with you, of being yours, and every time, I woke up alone. I just want to make sure I'm not hallucinating all of this," I admitted sheepishly. My cheeks flushed with both passion and embarrassment.

"You weren't dreaming alone," he murmured, and I was glad I wasn't standing because I suspected my knees might have given out. His lips curled into a wickedly handsome grin.

He dipped to kiss me again, and while his soft, urgent lips moved with mine, his hands coursed up and down my body, heating me as he touched every part of me that ached for him. I arched my back and moaned, relishing in the reality of his touch, no longer a fantasy.

When his hand snaked beneath the hem of the dress

I wore and slipped higher and higher up my thighs until it reached the very center of my need for him, my breath caught and I struggled to find words. I was gasping with desire.

"I–I," I stammered.

"Yes?" He growled into my neck as he kissed me, showering me with sensual grazes of his lips.

My eyes fluttered closed, soaking in the sensation, until his fingers parted me, touching me where I'd never been touched before, shocking the truth out of me. I groaned with passion.

"I've never done . . . this," I managed. His head lifted and his eyes searched mine, and I sputtered, "I mean, I want to. I've dreamed of it a thousand times." I sighed and blushed simultaneously. "I just, I'm not *quite* a hundred percent sure what I'm doing." I chuckled apprehensively, even though I was burning with desire for him.

He smiled and lowered his head to my neck, licking the sensitive spot just beneath my ear lobe, then pulled back and studied my face. "We have a saying on Trilynia. 'Love makes all things new, and all things rough, turned smooth.'" His fingers trailed along my neck and over the rise of my breast. "All things broken made whole, all things dormant shall bloom, all things right, with two hearts so full."

"That's lovely," I murmured, infatuated with him.

"Tonight, my heart *is* full, and everything between us . . . I've never known love like this. To me, it is new as well," he whispered as he raised my fingers to his lips, kissing each one individually. I giggled and squirmed, relishing in his attention focused directly on me. He was pouring himself out to me, wearing his heart on his sleeve.

Never having swooned before, the feeling was unfamiliar, but for a moment, everything went a little blurry and out of focus. And then I felt his lips at mine once more and surrendered to the demanding aches of my body. It was a natural bliss that I gave in to with awe and captivation.

Peeling my dress carefully off me, his mouth found every inch of skin and claimed it as his. Lying bare before him, I reached out and slid my hands inside the collar of his robes, needing to feel him against me with nothing, not even a thin scrap of fabric, between us. Heat formed between us, igniting a flame of passion and raw desire.

My hand brushed against his hardness as I pulled the clothing off him, and I gasped, surprised and unsure.

He didn't push me, just watched as I explored him with my fingers, tracing the firm line of him, gripping it as the persistent throb pulsed in my hand. His breathing hitched and his eyes glazed as I tenderly stroked, committing every glorious reaction to memory. His girth was profound, wonderful.

Finally, he gripped my wrist and pinned me back, arms above my head, as he parted my legs with his thick thighs and the slick head of him nudged against me. I felt him pulsing with longing. My own insides were pulsing with a burning need for him too.

"I think you got the hang of that just fine." He grinned as he lowered his mouth to the taut peak of my breast. His breath was icy and hot, a perfect blend against my sensitive, fiery skin.

Releasing my hands, he lowered his own to my center, his long, thick fingers stroking and parting me. When one dipped inside, I felt the sweet tremble of sensation ripple through every muscle. My mouth parted with a soft and sensual moan.

My fingers wound into the dense black forest of his hair, gripping harder and harder as his fingers stoked the coiling pleasure inside me. My breath came in pants, my body heated, and my senses fogged as he focused his efforts at the tight center of my nerves, rubbing in persistent, unrelenting circles until I felt my muscles tense.

In the same instant, everything in me shuddered with release as he brought me to the peak and filled me all at once. My thirst was wild, surging into overdrive.

If there was pain, I was too delirious to register it as he stroked slowly in and out. The ecstasy didn't abate as he moved with firm control, slowly at first and then with growing speed. Each thrust made me gasp. He was thick and filled me with amazing comfort.

"You burn me," he gasped as my senses began to crest again, and I moaned his name, sensually running my trembling hands through his hair once again.

Then, with one last surging thrust, my body tensed and gripped him as pleasure rocketed through us both. Fireworks pulsed in my eyes. Ripples of ecstasy shuddered through me as I cried out, releasing my sweet nectar all over his hardness.

My breathing was still broken when he withdrew from me, leaving an unfamiliar wet sensation that made me blush and aroused me at the same time. I was vulnerable, and I loved every second of it. Gardax had taken me. Our relationship had burst through to the next level.

Collapsing beside me, he nuzzled close, and basking

in the glow of what we'd just shared, our breathing slowed. I waited until I could hear our hearts beating in unison. It was incredibly peaceful.

He tangled his fingers into my hair, now a collapsed mass of curling waves. His cheeks were flushed in the afterglow of the love we'd just shared.

"I never want to lose you again," he said, his voice raspy and strangled with emotion. He nestled up beside me and squeezed me gently.

"You never did," I murmured as I kissed him. I knew it, deep inside. I always knew we belonged together, even if the world had desperately tried to keep us apart.

IT MUST HAVE STILL BEEN NIGHT. I COULDN'T TELL and didn't care. All that mattered was that when I woke, I wasn't alone. The weight of Gardax's arm slumped over my waist and around my front, holding me firmly against him. I would never have to wake up alone, hungry, or cold again.

His breathing was even and slow, and I smiled, reveling in the rare and incredible feeling of home. I belonged here with him. It was slowly sinking in.

This was the placed I'd longed for, the satisfaction, the belonging that I'd never felt, not even in dreams. I still wanted to pinch myself in disbelief that this was all really happening.

I carefully wiggled around to face him, hoping not to wake him, and studied his face, touching his cheek as lightly as I could. Gently, I dragged my fingers along the defined muscles of his biceps, his massive shoulders, and along the ridges of his abs. His body was my sensual pleasure center. I wanted to explore and discover every crevice.

"And what do you think you're doing?" he said, eyes still closed, but a smile curled at the edges of his lips.

I smiled and bit my lip, blushing even though he couldn't see it. "Enjoying the view," I whispered sensually.

"I may not know everything about human physiology, but I think I know enough to determine you don't see with your hands," he said, rolling on top of me with a sudden swiftness I didn't expect.

"What do I do with my hands then?" I teased and giggled seductively.

"Hmm," he said, rolling my hard nipple between his thumb and forefinger. "I think I'll need to do some research on the matter and get back to you. It is our wedding night, after all."

"Ah, yes," I gasped as he licked a trail from my breast to my navel. "I suppose we have a job to do." I gasped at his touch. His lips perfectly grazed against my bare tummy.

"What's that?" he asked, his voice vibrating against my hip.

"Well, we've got a planet to repopulate, right?" I managed as his fingers slipped inside me. I was already puddling for him, expectantly waiting for bliss to consume me.

He laughed and rose back up to my face. "How very royal of you, to be so preoccupied with your duty."

Feeling suddenly full of sensual confidence, I hooked my leg around his calf and nudged, rolling on top of him in one quick movement that sent him falling backward against the pillows. He stared up at me as if he was enjoying the view and intoxicated by my body.

Then, climbing up and straddling the part of him that was hard and swollen just for me, I smiled. "I'm a very hard worker, trust me."

MORNING CAME, AND IT TOOK EVERYTHING IN ME to get out of bed, especially when Gardax kept pulling me back in. So, I let him. Twice. I couldn't stop. I was already addicted to his passionate love-making. He had skills, and it felt so natural to be with him.

By the third time that morning, and . . . what? The fourth, fifth, or who knows what round we were on since we'd married the night before, I needed to make sure my legs still worked. I was wobbly and creamy all over.

Gardax showed me the cleansing chamber and just how erotic washing could be. We were lathered up together, bodies pressed against each other. Soapy and sensual, warm, and full of erotic bliss.

But when we climbed out, clothed in thick, fluffy towels and ready to dry each other off, reality invaded our happy bubble. Our relationship and our marriage wouldn't always be sunshine and roses and love-making in bed all day.

There were still matters to be dealt with, the most pressing of which was named Darla. She was still awaiting a sentence for her crimes. Every time I thought about what disgusting things she'd put me and Corinne through, bile rose in my throat.

Gardax's secretary had sent me a selection of Trilyn robes and garments that rivaled the beauty of the dress Darbnix had given me. Unaccustomed to such finery, I selected something a bit simpler, promising myself that I'd work toward wearing the more elaborate, intricate fashions with time.

I slipped into a velvety plum dress that draped and hung in ways I didn't think clothing *could* on my body, and which, Gardax promised, wouldn't last on it very long once we were done with necessary business for the morning.

I checked in first with Corinne, who demanded to know every detail of my wedding night and with whom I shared none. I laughed as she proudly proclaimed herself psychic for having predicted that she would be lavished with servants and food galore while I went off and made lots of little princes and princesses.

She was already showing signs of recovery. Her cheeks had a healthy, rosy tint to them, and she was becoming more of her witty self once again. She was in moral, healing hands, and I trusted the medical team handpicked by Gardax.

Satisfied that she was being well cared for, I also checked on Bodi.

"Well, looks like things worked out for ya." He smiled, though I could sense the vulnerable child beneath. He gave me a simple smile that was laced with the innocence of his youth.

"They really did." I smiled. "Look, I was thinking. I know you said you wanted to head to San Clemente, right?" I asked.

He nodded a little sadly. "Yep, warm weather and me just make sense." He shrugged humbly and met my gaze.

"Well, Gardax tells me it's warm on Trilynia too. You could come with us, unless you're set on San Clemente," I said innocently, as if the thought just occurred to me. I gave him a warm smile. The offer was out there. All he had to do was accept.

Bodi looked at me like I was crazy. "Why would you want that?"

I looked at him earnestly and explained, "I was on my own at your age—well, mostly. I had a four-year-old sister to take care of. But I know what it's like to feel alone. It's a hard life, and if you're not careful, it'll break you down. You've got a lot of potential, you know, and you had my back when no one else did. I figure, I'm going to a new place where I don't really know anyone. Might be nice for someone to have my back there too."

I just wanted to give him options. I knew we could help offer him a better life if he came with us. I felt a need to protect him, just like I did with Corinne.

He smiled skeptically. "So you're saying you need protection? There's a lot of hulking guards around here who would suggest otherwise."

"No, I'm saying I need a friend. And maybe an e-scrapper, a savant, a jack of all trades, etcetera." I smiled. I was trying to compliment him into agreeing.

"You forgot male model," he reminded me.

I laughed. He was funny. I had to hand it to him. "Don't push your luck, kid. You in?"

He made a show of rolling his eyes and acting like it was no big deal, but the glistening at his eyes told me otherwise. "Yeah, okay, sure. Could be cool." Inside, I knew that he was probably jumping for joy. He just didn't know how to express it.

"Cool," I agreed as we shook hands. It was a deal.

"ARE YOU READY?" GARDAX ASKED, SLIPPING HIS hand into mine as we walked through the still confusing maze of passages.

I squeezed. "Very." I was poised and calmer than I expected to be.

We entered the small chamber. To the far side was a long rectangular cell, outfitted with reasonably comfortable furniture. Lying on the simple bed was Darla, still in the red dress that was practically painted onto her from the night before, her hair a ratty tangle of dirty blonde.

When we came in, she sat up and looked at us, wild-eyed like a caged animal. Her eyes frantically darted between us as if she were skeptical and distrusting.

"What the hell do you want?" she growled, edging away from us and backing herself into a corner.

Gardax tensed. I felt the muscles of his arm stiffen and strain, but I put a hand to his arm and stepped forward to the front of Darla's cell.

"I wonder what must have happened to you. What awful thing did you go through that turned you into this horrible, hateful creature?"

She spat at the floor. "Keep your pity, you trash. I don't need anything from you."

I laughed humorlessly. "You always thought me such an easy target for your tyranny, your cruel abuse and torment. But you see, I was not the meek, wilting flower you thought. You don't want my pity? That's fine, because you don't have it. I'm not here to offer my pity, my sympathy, or my forgiveness," I said calmly.

She looked up then, eyeing me suspiciously with eyes full of loathing and jealousy.

"Then what the bloody fuck *did* you come here for?" she hissed.

I smiled. "I came to offer you an invitation."

"A what—" she stuttered, glancing at Gardax as if she couldn't believe what she was hearing.

"To our wedding feast. Trilynian tradition calls for a public wedding feast. You are invited, though you'll be accompanied by a guard, of course. But I very much look forward to your dancing in celebration with us."

She slinked forward, hate and disgust in her eyes. "I will never dance for you," she whispered as she looked away.

I turned back and held Gardax's hand once more. "Oh, but I think you will. And you had best dance well if you don't wish to lose your feet." My tone was laced with warning. The ball was in my court. Finally, I had the upper hand against Darla's abuse.

THE RETURN VOYAGE TO TRILYNIA WOULD TAKE several months, but it was hard to note the passing time when we so rarely left our bedroom.

As I relaxed into sleep with my new husband, far away from the world that had treated me so callously, and rocketed toward a world in dire need of hope, I looked down at his large hand upon my stomach and wondered what new worlds we were forming there together.

Whatever—whoever—grew within me, I knew Gardax was right. Love makes all things new.

What we shared, what we'd created together, it had made me new. I couldn't wait to start our future together, but for now, I was elated to be in the present with him, never leaving each other's side.

ABOUT ZARA ZENIA

Zara Zenia writes steamy, sexy, and suspenseful sci-fi romances! You will find her writing alien romances from intergalactic planets, bionic romances, super-heroes and time travel romances too.

Please see her Author Central Account on Amazon for a full list of her titles.

Sign up for her mailing list and find out about her latest releases, giveaways, and more. Also get a free book! Click here!

For more information, be sure to check out the links below!

zarazenia.com
zara@zarazenia.com

Aliens of Dragselis Series:

Zaruv: A Sci-Fi Alien Dragon Romance (Book 1)

Karun: A Sci-Fi Alien Dragon Romance (Book 2)

Ragal: A Sci-Fi Alien Dragon Romance (Book 3)

Pavar: A Sci-Fi Alien Dragon Romance (Book 4)

Rizor: A Sci-Fi Alien Dragon Romance (Book 5)

❧

Royally Blue - Celestial Mates:

Blue Alien Prince's Mate: A Sci-Fi Alien Romance
(Celestial Mates)

Alien Gladiator's Mate: A Sci-Fi Alien Romance (Celestial
Mates)

The Blue Alien's Mate: A Sci-Fi Alien Romance (Celestial
Mates)

Blue Alien Prince's Captive Bride: A Sci-Fi Alien Romance
(Celestial Mates)

Blue Alien Prince's Mail-Order Bride: A Sci-Fi Alien

Romance (Celestial Mates)

***

Trilyn Fairy Tales Series:

Alien Prince Charming (Book 1)

***

Reverse Harem Romance Series:

Fire, Blood, and Beauty (Book 1)

Fangs, Flames, and Allure (Book 2)

***

Alien Abduction Series:

Alien Zookeeper's Abduction (Book 1)

Alien Mate's Abduction (Book 2)

Alien Captive's Abduction (Book 3)

***

Alien Auction House Series:

Sold To The Alien King (Book 1)

Bought By The Alien Prince (Book 2)

Warriors of Orba Series:

Standalones:

ZARUV PREVIEW

Preview:

Book 1 of the Aliens of Dragselis Series: <u>Zaruv: A Sci-Fi Alien Dragon Romance</u>

CHAPTER 1-ZARUV

Pavar glared at Karun while nodding in respect toward his elder brother. "We are heading to Artax, where we are sentenced to live out our lives away from our home and our people but you still support the rule?"

"I do," replied Karun confidently. "The system, though flawed, has worked well long before we were here. It will continue to work long after we are gone."

"You make Artax sound like a prison," I interjected. "Artax is a resort planet, dear brother. We are going to live out our lives with more Dragselian woman and servants than we can handle. Yet you seem to find a way to make it sound terrible."

"That's because it is! I want to be back home on Dragselia, not billions of light years away from it."

"You are so ready to start a fight when our father has not even been dead a week. You mourn the loss of your comfort, but not the man who provided it. You should be ashamed, Pavar," Ragal said.

My two brothers sat down at the table with myself and Pavar. Looking around at them I saw the stark differences between them. Each one of them had a different personality that had its flaws, but also its winning qualities. I could think of no better warrior than Karun. His strength, speed, and agility were almost matched with my own. An anger boiled below the surface though. He hated the exile even more than Pavar, though his loyalty to the Dragselian way ran deeper than his disdain.

"We are not far from Artax now, I think you will sing a new song once you see what waits for us there, Pavar," Karun said

"Karun, you won't win. I would encourage you to let it go now before a war of our own starts," interjected Ragal.

"I agree," I said while nodding to Ragal. "There is nothing that we can do about it now. Pavar, you may voice your concerns among us brothers, but once we reach Artax, there will be no room for that hostility."

"Why not?" Pavar fumed.

I started to speak, but it was again Ragal who answered. "Because Artax is a haven of Dragselian. To speak against your king would be unforgivable."

"Maybe that's what I need to do then, at least I wouldn't be living a lie."

Karun sighed and shook his head, "Then we will be forced to live with your death. You will be painted the selfish, spoiled brat that you are."

Pavar leaped up, but I raised my hand in a command for him to sit. He begrudgingly listened. This wasn't the first time that he'd tried to start a fight in the close quarters and I knew it wouldn't be the last. I didn't worry about Ragal. His level head and passive nature wouldn't allow him to partake in such a point-less fight. It was the others that I was worried about. Karun was a fighter and Pavar was an instigator but

Ragal only wanted peace to reign out over all others. I smiled at him as he sat silently, looking out at the stars as they flew past us.

"We are close," Ragal whispered beneath Pavar and Karun's argument.

I looked out the front window and took in the beauty of the planet. It had been many years since I'd ventured to the area. Everything seemed the same. A small flicker of light caught my eye. At first, I thought that it was a star, but it seemed to be moving. Another ship in this area was common. Artax was a popular resort planet. No chime of the security console came but that did little to comfort me. It was programmed to send a message to all ships in our area, keep track of their level of danger.

Our vessel did not bear the royal insignia of our home planet. It was too dangerous to openly declare that there were royals on board. Throughout the area, there were Infernians lurking and waiting for our capture and eventual death. If no heirs to the throne were alive, they could easily overthrow our rule. I kept a watchful eye on the ship. It wouldn't take much to fool our system. A false sense of security might blanket those who didn't know the price on our heads, but it did little to put my mind at ease.

"What troubles you, brother?" Ragal asked, watching the changes of my face.

I shook my head, not wanting to alert the others of potential danger until I was sure. "It's nothing, just my paranoid mind playing tricks on me. I think that I, too, am getting a little stir crazy."

Ragal smiled and leaned back, "I believe it's infected me as well. I will be glad when I can again rest my feet on solid ground."

I snickered, Ragal hated to be on ships. The uncertainty of the unknown did little to comfort him. He was not one for adventure. Left alone with his charts and the stars, he was a very happy nomad. I glanced back at the window, searching for the small blinking light. At first, I thought it had gone, moved onto whatever planet it was destined for, but then I caught it again, this time it was closer and worse, it wasn't alone.

My heart started to race, wondering if it was enough danger to alert the others. In my hesitation to speak though, a heavy silence fell over the cabin. Karun and Pavar were no longer arguing with each other. The silence had transformed into a heavy fog, waiting for me to speak and lift it. I glanced back at the approaching ships, four in total and knew that I needed to make a decision. They would be on us in a matter of minutes.

"Zaruv?" Karun asked, "What troubles you?"

I looked him in the eyes, dark and brooding as always. We were an incredibly attractive lot by human standards. Our bodies had little to no hair, save for our heads which flowed freely down our backs, mine in waves of deep auburn. My heart was racing; we were not prepared for a fight as we flew in a passenger vessel with no security. Instantly, I regretted my decision to not push for some sort of escort. These were troubling times for our kind, as evident by the unmarked ships now closing in.

Karun saw them before I responded to him, "Are they Infernian ships?"

I shook my head, "There is no way to know. They do not have any markers or colors. I don't think they are coming to be friends though. Jartex?"

A computer voice rang out over our heads. Jartex was our security system. "Yes, my prince?"

"Can you send them a message please and ask that they identify themselves?"

"Shall I share make your royal presences known?" Jartex asked.

"No," I whispered. "Do not share who we are with them."

The four of us stood watching through the window as the ships grew closer. They couldn't see us through the thick glass, but we could see enough that my heart sank to the pit of my stomach. No passenger vehicle carried the two heavy missile portals on either side, as were the ships that were now hovering a few hundred feet from us. There was little doubt in my mind that they knew who was on board.

"Sir?" said Jartax, "They do not respond to my signal. Should I try again?"

I shook my head and took a step backward, tugging Pavar and Ragal along with me. "No Jartax, it's too late."

My three brothers looked to me, then back to the ships now facing us. They saw the same thing that I did, the missiles being lowered by long, metallic, arms as they prepared to fire. I could feel my stomach flipping in anticipation for a split second before I reacted.

"Jartax, drop range now!" I screamed out.

My brothers scurried around and quickly buckled into the seats around the emerald table, but Pavar wasn't fast enough. Our ship dropped from the dark sky and Pavar was shot up in the air, his back cracking against the ceiling. He quickly recovered, our bones and skeletal structure being stronger than that of humans. In our dragon forms, we were almost impossible to kill but shifting now would rip apart the small craft, sending us floating pointlessly into space.

"Take evasive measures!" I called out.

Karun quickly unbuckled and took the seat next to me as the autopilot engaged and started to dodge the incoming missiles.

"We need to get to the escape pods," Karun said.

I shook my head, "This far from Artax, we would never make it."

"What other options do we have? We cannot fight back; we are too far to call for help from home. It's the only chance that we have for survival."

An argument rose to my lips, but before I could share, the ship started to shake violently. One of the missiles had made contact, sending everything on the vessel flying through the air as we struggled to breathe through the debris and depleting oxygen. I nodded to Karun. He grabbed ahold of Pavar and I did the same to Ragal, shoving each one into an escape pod.

Before shutting the doors on the pods, I looked over at Karun and yelled, "Make for Vaxivia, I will find you all there."

Karun nodded, as did Pavar and Ragal before we sealed them in. Within seconds we heard the alarm of an incoming missile and quickly we both dove into our escape pods. Looking around at my brothers, I hit the eject button and was sent soaring into space. Unequipped for long travel, the air in the pod grew thin just as we entered Vaxivia's thin atmosphere.

The last memory I had before the darkness consumed me, was of my brothers. All I could do was hope that their fates had not yet ended. They were all the family I had left; someone had told the enemy where we were. There was a spy among our kind.

CHAPTER 2-JENNIFER

"Shh, Susan. Just one more and you will be all done," I cooed to the small girl.

Her pin-straight hair fell in clumps on her cheeks. She was covered in mud. Dark streaks crisscrossed her face from where she had tried in vain to wipe away the tears. The cut was deep, but short, thankfully. She needed a few stitches, but nothing I couldn't handle. It wasn't often that I'd come across an injury that my small, but well-equipped outpost clinic couldn't cover.

"Thank you so much, Jennifer," whispered Carla, Susan's mother.

I smiled up at her, covering the new sutures with a bandage. "It's no problem, Carla. I'm just happy you caught me before I headed home for the day. Otherwise, we would have had to cut it off."

Susan rolled her eyes at me but smiled, "You wouldn't do that to me."

I grinned at the little girl and reached behind me, producing a small, wrapped, red candy. "You're right. I could never do that to my favorite patient. Promise me you will stay away from the dunes from now on though, okay?"

Susan nodded her head and jumped down, her eyes glued on the candy prize in her hand. I pulled Carla aside while Susan was distracted. The little girl wasn't out of the woods yet. I couldn't count the number of injuries I saw because of the dunes. Vaxivia was no place to let your child wander outside of the outpost limits. There hadn't been a war in decades, but the very planet itself was a death trap unless you knew your way around it. No five-year-old should be wandering alone.

"You will need to watch for an infection. The dunes hold sand that can eat away at the skin."

Carla folded her hands nervously in her lap, "Okay. I know she shouldn't have been out there. I will be dealing with Michael when I get home."

"He's only eight, Carla. You know he shouldn't be left alone with her all day. Isn't there anyone who can help you out?"

She shook her head, "Please don't tell the guards. I promise I won't let it happen again."

I took her hands into mine. Her story was all too common. Work on Vaxivia was hard to find. Often the men of the family left to find work and never came back. Some still sent money back home, but many, like Carla's husband, were ghosts in the wind. She worked part time at the small diner to make ends meet, but childcare was just too expensive. My heart ached for her and the plight that she was in.

"Why don't you send her here tomorrow? I have some things she can do around the clinic and I can keep an eye on her wound."

"Really? She won't get in the way?"

I smiled at Susan who was still looking at her foil wrapped trophy. Running a clinic wasn't easy. The last thing I needed was a young girl running under foot. Still, I couldn't live with myself if something happened to her.

"She will be fine, I promise."

Carla thanked me all the way to the door. I knelt to speak to Susan, "Are you going to come help me tomorrow?"

She nodded her head and ran after her mom with more joy in her eyes than I'd ever seen. As I was standing up, I saw Mikey Jones running toward me at full speed. At once my heart jumped. He never ran that fast. Slight in build, Mikey was ten going on forty. Like all the young boys in the community, he had far too much weight on his young shoulders. I turned the clinic sign over to 'Closed' and grabbed my medical bag. I met him at the old hoverboard parked on the road.

"Jennifer! Jennifer!" he called to me. "There's an alien ship crashed outside of the outpost!"

The blood drained from my face at once, as I quickly glanced around. I didn't see Courtney's nosey eyes peering through her curtains. The last thing I needed was her running around and telling the guards that we had an alien. Not when I couldn't be sure that Mike was right. I jumped and covered his mouth with my hand. His eyes briefly shifted to fear before he nodded his head. I winced at his fear. I had momentarily forgotten about the abuse his bastard father had inflicted on him before he skipped town.

"Okay Mikey, we will go take a look but you've got to keep your voice down, okay?"

He nodded his head, "Sorry, Jennifer. I'm so stupid. I forgot."

I winced again, "Mikey, you are far from stupid. I don't want to hear you talk like that about yourself ever again, okay? I just don't want everyone to know about the alien just yet."

"Got it, I will be more careful," he whispered.

Nodding, I pressed my thumb against the scanner and the hovercraft slowly roared to life. It needed to be replaced years ago, but the money just wasn't there anymore. It shook and rattled as it lifted off the ground. I waited there for a few more seconds, giving it a chance to warm up. Once it was about a foot from the ground I pushed the handlebar forward and we started to move briskly through the streets. Within seconds we were coming up on the outpost wall. I glanced at the two guards and sighed. This was going to be tricky.

"Mikey?" I asked my passenger. "You are going to

hear me lie okay? I don't want them to know what you've found until I know it's safe."

He nodded his head and said nothing. I knew that he wouldn't say anything to the contrary to what I was going to say. He was another good kid tossed into a bad situation. His father wasn't missing though, he was buried in the small outpost cemetery, a victim of the dunes. With two younger sisters and a working mother, he would run errands for me and I would slip him any payment I could. Whether it was drupees or food, he was grateful for it all the same.

As I slowed to a stop, the younger of the two men sauntered over to me. I had to resist the urge to roll my eyes. Instead, I plastered a smile on my face. He was the last person I wanted to deal with knowing how the heavyset man felt about me. My numerous rejections of his advances never seemed to dull his attraction to me. No matter how one-sided it seemed to be. It was the same story with most of the other single men in the outpost. I didn't want to deal with any of them. The pool wasn't very deep on Vaxivia.

"How are you doing Zach?" I asked casually.

He winked at me, leaning against the hoverboard. "I'm doing a whole lot better now that you are visiting, Jennifer."

"Well, unfortunately, this isn't a social visit. I need to get out to the Jones' homestead. One of the girls has a bit of the flu. I just want to check on her to clear my mind."

He glanced around the hoverboard and saw Mikey for the first time. His mood changed at once. As soon as he realized he wasn't the center of my attention I knew that he was going to be a hard sell.

Zach shook his head, "No can do, Jennifer. We got word today that there might be hostiles in the area. Aren't supposed to let anyone in or out."

I gritted my teeth and batted my eyes. Letting my fingers trail off the controls and over to his. He twitched but didn't move his hand. His eyes lit up and a wide, white grin crossed his face.

"That's a shame. I was hoping to slip out there real fast, then be back at Sammy's by quitting time," I whispered.

He cleared his throat, the smile still on his face. I hated to lie but I knew if he thought I would be at the local pub later, he would let me go. He waved to the man at the gate and they slowly started to open.

"Thank you," I whispered to him.

He winked at me, "You can thank me later, honey."

My cheeks flushed red but not out of admiration. I didn't like having the attention of any man, least of all him. Blushing was my defense mechanism but he didn't need to know that. My skin felt like it was crawling from where I'd touched him. I was suddenly grateful for the sterilizing solution I had in my bag. I gave him one last smile as I slowly pulled through the gates and let them close behind me. As soon as I rounded the forest and I was out of sight, I pushed the throttle as hard as it would go.

"Where did you see it?" I asked Mikey once we were finally clear.

He pointed to a clearing in the forest, one that hadn't been there before. It didn't take me long to realize that the clearing was the aftermath of a large wreck. My stomach started to flutter. I couldn't believe that Mikey was telling the truth. He wasn't prone to lying, but your eyes could play tricks on even the most discerning child, especially one with a wild spirit like him. I swallowed hard and followed the trail. The closer we crept to the wreckage, the more I was regretting my decision to bring Mikey with me.

"Whatever you do, stay behind me. Do you understand?" I asked him as we parked.

He nodded his head, ducking between my arms and trying to see the wreckage. I'd never seen a ship like it before. It wasn't large, maybe a few dozen meters in width without its wings. I briefly glanced around but didn't see the wings anywhere.

"Why don't you go find the wings and other wreckage for me. I don't know what we are going to find when we open the hull, okay?"

Mikey nodded and disappeared off into the woods. The black craft was badly damaged, looking more like an ancient, buried torpedo than a ship. I looked for a door, following a trail of steam as it seeped from a thin seam. Still in shock that Mikey hadn't been lying, my attention turned to determining if there were any survivors. I was no stranger to aliens, but I kept my small gun close at my side just in case. The ship wasn't an Infernian vessel, that much was evident.

A low whistle escaped the pod and I stumbled backward, watching in stunned silence as the seam widened as a door opened. In a puff of smoke, the door creaked back on its dented hinges and my mouth fell open. There was someone inside of the pod, and from the small hole poking through the fumes, I could see a man's chest slowly moving up and down.

"Thank God," I whispered. He was alive.

When the last of the smoke cleared, I was once again stunned into silence. There wasn't much blood, less than I had expected. What gave me pause was the alien's stunning looks. His body was rugged and muscular, with olive-toned skin that I could see where his uniform had torn open. Swallowing back my words, I let my gaze travel up his body to his face. Though his eyes were closed, I could only imagine the beauty that they would behold, if they matched the rest of his figure.

His dark, auburn, hair fell loose down to his shoulders. A strong jaw and thickly lashed eyes rounded out one of the most attractive faces I'd ever seen. When a groan slipped past his lips, I jumped. As his head listlessly turned to the side, I saw the reason he was unconscious. A gaping wound cut through the side of his head. I quickly pushed my fear and wonder aside and reached into my medical bag. Any emotions that I had before were now gone. He was injured and nothing else mattered but keeping him alive.

"Mikey!" I called out.

The child was at my side in a flash. I looked deeply into his eyes, praying there would be enough strength to lift the alien between the two of us.

"We have to get him back to my apartment, and fast," I whispered to him.

Click <u>HERE</u> to continue reading book 1 of the Aliens of Dragselis series, <u>Zaruv: A Sci-Fi Alien Dragon Romance</u> if you haven't already!

Made in the USA
Monee, IL
10 January 2020